FROM THE
NANCY DREW FILES

THE CASE: Nancy searches for a runaway bride and
finds a secret worth killing for.

CONTACT: Midori Kato was scheduled to take a
walk down the aisle . . . but instead took a detour
into danger.

SUSPECTS: Ken Nakamura—*The bridegroom-to-be
is in line to take over Nakamura Inc.—a powerful
company whose secrets must be protected at any
cost.*

Yoko Nakamura—*Ken's mother has always ob-
jected to the marriage and may have found a way
to terminate the engagement . . . permanently.*

"Mad Dog" Hayashi—*A fellow art student whose
interest in Midori may have extended beyond the
classroom into an obsession. . . .*

COMPLICATION: *In order to investigate Nakamura Inc., Nancy enlists an employee, old friend
Mick Devlin, to pose as her boyfriend. But the
longer the masquerade lasts, the more real the
romance seems . . . and Ned is thousands of
miles away.*

Books in The Nancy Drew Files® Series

Available from ARCHWAY Paperbacks

The Nancy Drew Files™

Case 96
The Runaway Bride
Carolyn Keene

AN ARCHWAY PAPERBACK
Published by POCKET BOOKS
New York   London   Toronto   Sydney   Tokyo   Singapore

AN ARCHWAY PAPERBACK *Original*

An Archway Paperback published by
POCKET BOOKS, a division of Simon & Schuster Inc.
1230 Avenue of the Americas, New York, NY 10020

Copyright © 1994 by Simon & Schuster Inc.
Produced by Mega-Books of New York, Inc.

ISBN: 0-671-79488-4

First Archway Paperback printing June 1994

10 9 8 7 6 5 4 3 2 1

NANCY DREW, AN ARCHWAY PAPERBACK and colophon are registered trademarks of Simon & Schuster Inc.

THE NANCY DREW FILES is a trademark of Simon & Schuster Inc.

Cover art by Cliff Miller

Printed in the U.S.A.

IL 6+

Chapter

One

GEORGE FAYNE POINTED out the window of the taxi, which was crawling through traffic along a congested Tokyo highway. "Am I seeing things, Nan, or is that a huge pink castle in the middle of all those skyscrapers?"

Nancy Drew brushed back a strand of reddish blond hair and peered over George's shoulder. "It's definitely a huge pink castle," she replied. "The sign either says 'The Princess Hotel' or 'Pickles Sold Here.'"

George whirled around to Nancy, looking alarmed.

"Hey, I'm just kidding," Nancy said with a grin.

"You had me worried," George murmured. "You know, Drew, I'm counting on you to get us through this trip. The only Japanese phrases I managed to memorize before we left River Heights were for 'Hello,' 'Goodbye,' 'Thank you,' and 'I have a really bad stomachache.'"

"A lot of Japanese people speak English, so we'll do fine," Nancy reassured her.

The girls fell silent as they turned back to take in the view. Nancy had been in Tokyo before, but its crowds and hubbub still amazed her. As they approached the heart of town, high-rises and storefronts were jammed together on every available inch of land. Hundreds of neon signs flashed brightly colored messages in Japanese and English. Peering out at the narrow streets mobbed with people, Nancy wondered how cars ever managed to move through them.

George pointed at a large patch of green in the distance. "Hey, a park," she said. "Do you think that could be where Midori and Ken are getting married?" Nancy and George had come to Japan to attend the wedding of Midori Kato, who'd been a close friend during her year as an exchange student at River Heights High School.

"I think their park's in a different part of Tokyo," Nancy said. "And it's not just any park—it's the grounds of the Hamada Imperial Villa. It used to be the summer home of a prince, but now it's owned by the Japanese government."

"Someone's been memorizing her travel guide," George teased, her dark eyes twinkling.

Nancy blushed slightly. "Midori told me about the villa when we talked on the phone last week."

The cabdriver abruptly braked to avoid colliding with the car in front of them. He spun around and apologized to the girls, who were clutching their seats.

"No problem," George said. Then she whispered to Nancy, "I wish all cabdrivers were this polite."

She fished a comb out of her purse and began fluffing out her short dark curls. "So Midori and Ken are getting married at an imperial villa, huh? The Katos must have awesome connections to line up a place like that."

"I think it's the Nakamuras who've got the connections," Nancy said. "Midori mentioned that Nakamura Incorporated is one of the biggest investment-banking firms in the country, and that it's got lots of clout with the government. Ken's dad used to run it, but after he died, his Uncle Seiji took over."

George tucked her comb back into her purse. "Ken works for his uncle, right?"

Nancy nodded. "I can't wait to meet him. He sounds like a great guy. Midori told me he sends her flowers once a week—isn't that romantic?"

George nodded. "I can't believe this is an arranged marriage. It's like something out of the nineteenth century, isn't it?"

"But it's very common in twentieth-century

Japan," Nancy said. "Besides, Midori feels very lucky. She's nuts about Ken."

George elbowed Nancy. "Don't tell me you wouldn't be mad if your dad suddenly announced that he'd picked out a husband for you."

Nancy shook her head as she tried to imagine it. "Ned wouldn't be very happy about it, either," Nancy said. Ned Nickerson was her steady boyfriend.

The taxi crept to a halt at a gridlocked intersection. Nancy leaned back in her seat and sighed. "This ride is endless, isn't it?"

"Speaking of endless, check out our cab fare," George said in a low voice. She pointed at the meter, which was clicking away. "I may be slow in the yen-to-dollar conversion department, but if that number gets any higher, we're going to be living on rice and water during our entire vacation."

It was after five o'clock when the cab pulled up in front of the Sakura Ryokan, a traditional Japanese inn tucked into a shady residential street in one of the older sections of Tokyo. Midori's parents had selected it and had made the girls' reservations.

"We're finally here!" George cried as they got out of the cab.

The *ryokan* was a narrow, three-story wooden building. A line of large flat rocks were laid across the tiny front yard as a walkway to the entrance, which was framed by a pair of trees. The sliding door was partially open.

Nancy and George stepped into the foyer, which was cluttered with rows of shoes of all shapes and sizes. Nancy pointed to a rack holding dozens of identical orange slippers. "I guess we wear those inside."

Just then a middle-aged woman came rushing toward them. She wore her silvery black hair in a bun at the nape of her neck, and her wide face was dotted with pale golden freckles.

She smiled graciously at the girls. *"Irasshaimasei,"* she said. "Welcome. You are Ms. Drew and Ms. Fayne? Please allow me to show you to your room. I am Mrs. Ito, the manager."

She led them upstairs to a large Japanese-style suite. The floor was covered with a straw tatami mat. The living room area, which consisted of a low lacquer table, dark blue floor cushions, and a television set, was separated from the sleeping area by paper and wood shoji screens. The only decoration was a calligraphy scroll on one wall. Under it were some white chrysanthemums in a shallow black dish.

"Please make yourselves comfortable," Mrs. Ito told Nancy and George. "I will get you some *ocha* and *osembei*—tea and seaweed-covered rice crackers." She left, closing the sliding door softly behind her.

George peeled off her jacket, frowning. "Did she say *seaweed*-covered rice crackers? I think I'll pass. They sound kind of slimy."

"The seaweed is dried, silly," Nancy said playfully. "You should at least try them." She glanced at her watch. "It's almost five thirty. Midori wanted us to drop by to meet her parents when we got in. She said their house is just a few blocks from here. Okay?"

George's face lit up. "Great. If we hurry, we can get out of here before Mrs. Ito comes back with the—"

Just then there was a light knock, the sliding door opened, and Mrs. Ito entered with a tray. "Tea and rice crackers," she announced cheerfully.

Nancy winked at George. "I'm sure the Katos can wait a few more minutes," she said merrily. "Come on, Fayne, dig in."

Nancy paused at the intersection of two quiet, tree-lined streets and stared intently at the piece of paper in her hand. "We turn right here. Midori said that it was a charcoal gray house with wooden shutters."

"I think I see it," George replied. "Come on, Nan."

As they walked, Nancy noted that most of the houses in Midori's neighborhood were stucco, with tiny yards enclosed by bamboo fences. Behind some of the fences she could make out laundry drying on clotheslines, flapping gently in the June breeze.

"I have to admit, I'm a little nervous about seeing Midori," George said. "It's been a while since we saw her."

"Don't worry," Nancy said, hooking her thumbs into her jeans pockets. "When I talked to her on the phone, she sounded just like she did in high school. You know—cracking jokes, gabbing a mile a minute."

"That's our Midori," George remarked, smiling. "Did you ask her about why she dropped out of art school?"

Nancy frowned thoughtfully. "She didn't mention it, although she did grill me about the art scene in Chicago. We mostly talked about her wedding—what she's wearing, things like that. I couldn't get a word in edgewise, she was so excited."

Two little girls popped out from behind one of the bamboo fences. "Hello," George said to them in Japanese. They looked at each other, giggled, and ran off down the street.

"So much for my Japanese," George said to Nancy, shrugging. "Anyway, tell me. What's Midori wearing?"

"A kimono," Nancy replied. "It's a family heirloom. I can't wait to see it. Bess made me promise that I'd take a picture." Bess Marvin was George's cousin and Nancy's other best friend. She'd been invited to Midori's wedding, too, but couldn't make it because she was in Maine with her parents.

George stopped in front of a gray house. "This must be it, don't you think?"

Nancy nodded, then went up to the front door and knocked. A moment later it was opened by a short woman with shoulder-length black hair and wire-rimmed glasses. She was wiping her hands briskly on a white apron.

"You must be Nancy and George," the woman said in nearly perfect English. Nancy noticed that she spoke very quickly, just as Midori did. "I'm Toshiko Kato, Midori's mother. Please come in—you must be tired after your long trip."

She led the girls to a spacious Japanese-style living room. A slim gray-haired man with a closely cropped mustache and beard was sitting at a low lacquer table, reading a newspaper.

He snapped the paper shut and put it down. "Ah, Midori's friends from America," he boomed. "I'm Tadashi Kato. Please, please, have a seat."

Midori's mother poured some green tea into brown earthenware cups and passed them around. "How was your flight?" she asked the girls.

Nancy accepted a cup of the tea and inhaled its pleasantly bitter fragrance. "It was long, but we're glad to be here. We wouldn't have missed Midori's wedding for anything." She glanced around. "Is Midori here? We're dying to see her."

Toshiko rose from the table and opened the sliding door. "Midori! Your friends are here!" she called out.

A few seconds later Nancy heard footsteps, and Midori walked in. She was just as Nancy remembered her, with a small upturned nose and black hair that fell softly around her face. She was dressed in white cutoffs and a paint-splotched T-shirt that said "Senagawa Art College" in English and in Japanese.

"Midori!" Nancy cried out, jumping up to hug her. George did the same.

"Hi," Midori said quietly. She let the girls hug her, then joined them at the table without another word.

An awkward silence followed. Nancy cleared her throat and said, "Our inn is lovely. Thank you for making the arrangements, Mr. and Mrs. Kato."

"It's no problem," Toshiko said. "We've known Mrs. Ito for many years. She used to baby-sit for Midori and her sister Mari when they were little—isn't that right, Midori?"

"What?" Midori murmured, raising her eyes from the table.

Nancy studied her Japanese friend. Her face was pale and her eyes were red. Had she been crying? Nancy wondered.

George, who obviously noticed the same thing, raised her eyebrows at Nancy, then turned to Midori. "Have you been working on your art?"

she asked brightly, pointing at Midori's paint-splotched T-shirt.

"Not really," the Japanese girl replied tonelessly, and stared into her cup of tea.

Nancy frowned. Her instincts told her that something was very wrong with Midori. She'd seemed fine on the phone the past week, but now she was acting as if her best friend had died.

Nancy decided to bring up a subject that was sure to cheer Midori up. "So, Midori, are you all ready for the big day? We can't wait to meet Ken."

To Nancy's surprise, her words had the opposite effect on Midori. She raised her head suddenly and stared at Nancy, her face deathly white and her amber eyes wide with anguish.

"Midori?" Nancy said in alarm. "Did I say something wr—"

Before Nancy could finish her sentence, Midori had burst into tears. She sobbed deeply for a second, then rose shakily and ran out of the room.

Chapter

Two

"MIDORI!" NANCY CALLED after her. She turned helplessly to the Katos. "I'm sorry, I didn't mean to upset her."

The Katos glanced at each other. Nancy thought they were acting almost as agitated as Midori had.

Toshiko sighed heavily. "It's nothing you said, Nancy. In fact, I hope you will forgive our daughter. This is no way for her to behave with her guests."

"Something's bothering her," George began. "She's definitely not her old self."

Tadashi stood up. "I'm going to have a word with her," he said. "She cannot treat her family and friends in this manner—and on the eve of her wedding, of all nights!"

11

After Tadashi left, Toshiko said, "We're as confused by her behavior as you are. She's been like this since last night. She had a date with Ken, and ended up coming home early. Maybe they had a fight."

Nancy heard the front door open and close. A moment later a girl came bounding into the living room, a rhinestone-studded denim book bag slung over one shoulder. She looked like Midori, except she was a few inches shorter and had a ponytail with bangs and glasses. Nancy guessed she was about sixteen.

"You must be Midori's sister Mari," George said. She introduced herself and Nancy.

Mari grinned. "It's good to meet you. Aside from Ken and the wedding, you're all Midori's been talking about lately."

Nancy was surprised to hear this. Midori's greeting had been anything but enthusiastic.

Mari sat down at the table and poured herself a cup of tea. "Where is Midori?" she asked her mother.

Toshiko told Mari about her older sister's sudden exit. "Your father's speaking to her now. Don't worry—she'll be fine."

Mari put her tea down, obviously troubled. "But, Mama—" she began.

"We mustn't burden our guests any further, Mari," Toshiko cut in tersely, then smiled at Nancy and George. The smile struck Nancy as forced. Toshiko was trying to cover up her anxiety about Midori. "Now, you girls must tell us what you do back in River Heights. Midori mentioned to us that you're a detective, Nancy."

George filled Mrs. Kato and Mari in on a few of Nancy's exploits. Mari was particularly interested in Nancy's detective work. The four of them chatted for a while, but when Nancy noticed George stifling a yawn, she decided it was time to go. They were both jet-lagged.

The sky was beginning to deepen into twilight as the girls walked back to their *ryokan*.

"What do you think was going on with Midori?" Nancy asked George.

"I don't know," George replied, stepping aside to let a restaurant delivery boy pass on his bicycle. The air filled briefly with the smells of ginger and soy sauce. "I guess it's prewedding jitters."

"I'm not so sure," Nancy said slowly.

George looked at her curiously. "What do you mean, Nan?"

"She sounded so happy in her letters, and during our phone call last week," Nancy pointed out. "Plus, she kept saying how excited she was about seeing us. And she hardly noticed us the whole time we were there! It was like she was on another planet."

They had reached their *ryokan*. A pink paper lantern hung above the front door, lighting the entryway.

George put a hand on Nancy's shoulder. "I

think your detective's instincts are working over-time. Midori's probably stressed out about the wedding. I bet she'll be fine by tomorrow."

"I guess you're right," Nancy said, then her blue eyes lit up. "Hey, I'm starving. Let's ask Mrs. Ito to recommend a Japanese noodle shop."

"Japanese noodles," George repeated slowly. "As long as they don't have any of that seaweed stuff in them, okay? I've had my quota for the day."

It was a picture-perfect Saturday morning in June as Nancy and George made their way across the grounds of the Hamada Imperial Villa—warm and balmy, with just a touch of a breeze. A few wispy clouds drifted lazily in an azure sky.

The Hamada Villa was a long, one-story wood-en structure decorated with gold paint and elabo-rate carvings of animals, gods, and goddesses. The low, sloping roof was covered with onyx black shingles.

Nancy and George followed the other wedding guests down a path of tiny, multicolored pebbles. It wound around from the front of the villa to the back, where the ceremony was to take place.

Along the way Nancy and George stopped frequently to admire the landscaping. There were flowers of every imaginable variety—purple irises, pink peonies, hundreds of roses. Red carp shimmered in small, lotus-filled ponds.

The pebbled walk ended at a high, semicircular

wooden bridge that arched over a slow-flowing brook. Nancy could see people in folding chairs beyond the bridge and hear occasional snatches of conversation and laughter.

"The reception will be in the villa afterward, right?" George asked Nancy as they crossed the bridge.

"A twelve-course banquet, Midori said." Nancy chuckled. "I'm glad we had a light breakfast."

The girls were making their way to their seats when Mari came up to them.

"Hi!" she said, smiling. She was dressed in a lavender silk suit and elbow-length white gloves.

"Hi, Mari," Nancy said. "How's Midori doing?"

Mari's smile faded. "I am not sure," she said doubtfully. "She is inside the villa right now. I have been helping her with her wedding kimono for the last three hours."

"Three hours!" George gasped.

Mari nodded. "It is incredibly complicated. There are slips and underslips and sashes. Anyway, she's all dressed now."

"Midori was really upset last night—" Nancy began.

"She has been like that for the last two days," Mari cut in tensely. "I wish I knew why. She will not talk to me about it. My parents say it is her nerves, but I am not sure. Just now she told me—"

She was interrupted by a deep, husky male

voice. "Mari, will you introduce me to your friends?"

Nancy turned to see a tall, cute guy in his early twenties moving toward them. He had a square, tan face, large brown eyes, and straight hair, which he wore long on top and short at the sides. He was dressed in a ceremonial black kimono embroidered with silver crests.

"Hi, Ken," Mari said, anxiety flashing briefly across her face.

Nancy could tell that Mari was wondering if Ken had overheard their conversation about Midori. Mari recovered her composure quickly. "Nancy, George, this is Kentaro Nakamura," she said smoothly. "Ken, this is Nancy Drew and George Fayne, Midori's friends from River Heights."

Ken extended his hand to each of the girls in turn. "It is a great pleasure to meet you," he said enthusiastically. "Midori has told me all about you. If you have the time, I'd like you to meet my family." He led them to three people who were standing nearby.

Nancy was struck by Ken's warmth as he introduced Nancy and George to his mother first. Yoko Nakamura was in her midforties. She had short jet black hair, high cheekbones, and a small, slim figure. Her elegant magenta suit and ruby and diamond necklace were obviously very expensive.

"You came all the way from America for the wedding?" Yoko said to the girls. She sounded amused. "How cute. Isn't that cute, Seiji?"

Seiji, the man Yoko was addressing, was a middle-aged version of Ken, with the same square face, tall, slender build, and deep, husky voice. His hair was streaked with gray, and he wore a pair of tiny rimless glasses.

He bowed to Nancy and George. "I am Ken's uncle, Seiji Nakamura," he said simply, ignoring his sister-in-law's remark.

"And this is Uncle Seiji's personal assistant, Connor Drake," Ken finished. Nancy and George shook hands with a stocky redheaded man in his twenties. He was dressed in a stylishly cut brown suit.

"How do you do," Connor said in a British accent. He glanced at the girls, then his pale gray eyes darted distractedly about the crowd. He was clearly not interested in them, Nancy realized.

Mari leaned toward Nancy and touched her elbow. "I am going to check on Midori," she whispered. "I will see you later." After bowing and exchanging a few words with the Nakamuras, she hurried off in the direction of the villa.

Seiji glanced at his watch. "It is almost time," he told his nephew.

"I had better go to my place," Ken said to Nancy and George. "Midori will kill me if I hold things up." His face was flushed and his eyes were bright with excitement.

"Good luck," Nancy called out as he, Seiji, Yoko, and Connor headed up the aisle. Then she and George found seats toward the back.

"Ken seems like a really sweet guy—not to mention a major hunk," George said to Nancy, crossing her legs and smoothing her green silk dress over her knees. "No wonder Midori's crazy about him."

There was a flurry of activity up front. Nancy noted that Yoko, Seiji, and Connor had taken seats in the front row. An elderly man in a dark kimono, who was probably the priest, was instructing Ken where to stand. A musician began to play the koto. The plaintive sound coming from the traditional wood and string instrument made Nancy think of ancient Japan.

"But Mrs. Nakamura's kind of a snob, if you ask me—and so is Connor," George continued. "Mr. Nakamura's okay, I guess—kind of quiet."

The girls continued to discuss the Nakamuras for a while. Then Nancy said, "I wonder what the delay is. It's after twelve."

"Weddings never start on time," George replied.

Another fifteen minutes passed, and still there was no ceremony. People were beginning to stir. Nancy noticed that Ken and the priest glanced toward the villa every few seconds. At one point Seiji got up from his seat and exchanged a few words with his nephew.

Just then Nancy spotted Midori's father approaching Seiji and Ken. After a moment Seiji shook his head and crooked his finger at Yoko, who rose from her seat. Then the four of them rushed off toward the villa.

"Something's up," Nancy said to George.

"Maybe Midori spilled tea on her kimono," George replied with a grin.

Nancy chuckled and glanced at her watch again. Twelve forty-five.

A blond guy sitting a few rows in front of her and George caught Nancy's attention. He was staring off to his right. Nancy could make out most of his handsome—and familiar—profile.

She took in a sharp breath. It couldn't be!

"What is it, Nan?" George demanded. "You look as if you've seen a ghost."

Nancy pointed to the guy, who was now facing front. "Am I crazy, or is that . . ."

Her words trailed off as she caught sight of Seiji walking briskly back from the villa and approaching the priest. They had a brief conversation. The koto music stopped, then Seiji stepped before the crowd and waved his hands. Yoko, Ken, Mari, and the Katos were nowhere to be seen.

"I think Mr. Nakamura's going to make an

announcement," George whispered apprehensively. "You'll have to translate for me. He doesn't look happy."

The crowd fell silent as Seiji bowed deeply.

He cleared his throat. "I regret to inform you that the wedding will not take place."

Chapter

Three

SEVERAL PEOPLE in the crowd gasped. Nancy and George stared at each other silently after Nancy translated.

"Please accept our humblest apologies," Seiji went on. "For those of you who need transportation back to downtown Tokyo or to the train station, we will arrange for limousines to take you there."

People began rising from their seats, whispering.

"I don't get it," George said to Nancy, not referring to the translation.

"I don't, either," Nancy replied grimly.

Then she spotted Mari near the villa. "Come on, George," she said, leaping up. "Maybe Mari can tell us what's going on."

21

They caught up with her just outside one of the back doors. "Mari!" Nancy called out.

Mari turned. Her face was streaked with tears.

Nancy put her hand on the girl's arm. "Are you okay?"

"I don't know," Mari moaned. "Everything is such a mess. My sister is gone!"

"What!" George cried out.

"Tell us what happened," Nancy said gently.

"After I left you and the Nakamuras, I went to find Midori," Mari explained shakily. "But she was not in her dressing room—she was nowhere in the villa! My parents and I searched for her, but we could not find her. When we told Mr. Nakamura, he said we would have to call off the wedding—"

"Could she have been kidnapped?" George said anxiously.

"I doubt that," Mari murmured. "I was trying to tell you earlier, before Ken interrupted us, that right before I left her Midori told me she would not go through with the wedding. I did not believe her. I thought it was just nerves." She began crying again. "I should have listened to my sister! Now she's gone!"

Nancy frowned. "Did she tell you why she didn't want to marry Ken?"

"No," Mari said, taking a lace handkerchief from her pocket and dabbing at her eyes. "My parents and the Nakamuras are saying that she ran away so she would not have to have an arranged marriage. They are all furious with her."

She put the handkerchief away and added, "But I know that Midori would never walk out on Ken. If she ran away, she had a good reason. She may be in some trouble."

Nancy's mind was reeling. She agreed with Mari. In all of her letters Midori had sounded so happy about marrying Ken. It was hard to believe that she'd try to get out of it, especially by running away.

Yet she couldn't forget Midori's behavior the night before—the way she'd burst out crying when Nancy brought up the subject of the wedding. What was going on? Had Midori exaggerated her affection for Ken in her letters?

Nancy turned to Mari. "What time did you leave Midori alone in her dressing room?"

"Approximately eleven thirty, I think," Mari replied, sniffling.

"And it was just before noon when you left us to check on her," Nancy went on. "We should question the staff of the villa before they leave. Someone may have seen Midori take off."

Mari clasped her hands and stared at Nancy imploringly. "Does this mean you will help me find her? You are a detective—you should be able to track her down!"

"I'd be glad to do what I can," Nancy replied. "Let's start inside the villa."

As the three girls headed down the main hall of

the old building in search of staff members, they passed the Katos, Seiji, and Connor in a large sitting room. The Katos and Seiji were having an argument. Connor was behind his boss, arms crossed, silent.

Mari rushed into the room. "What is going on?" she whispered to her mother, who raised a finger to her lips.

Nancy and George lingered just outside the doorway, not wanting to intrude. The argument was in Japanese, but Nancy managed to catch the gist of it.

"Your crazy daughter humiliated my family in front of hundreds of people!" Seiji was saying in a low, livid voice. "Yoko is so embarrassed she's hiding in one of the back rooms until all the guests have gone. And I don't even know where my nephew is."

"We had no idea Midori was planning to run away!" Tadashi replied, his face beet red. "She didn't tell us anything!" He turned to his wife. "It was that wild, free-thinking art school that did this to her, Toshiko. She used to be such an obedient girl. Now I don't know her."

"Papa, don't say that!" Mari cried out. "Midori's friend Nancy Drew is going to help us find her—"

"Find her!" Tadashi exclaimed. "Midori does not want to be found. She would not dare show her face after what she has done."

Toshiko put her hand on her husband's arm. "Tadashi, you are being too hard," she murmured.

"He is right, Toshiko," Seiji remarked. "Midori has brought disgrace to both of our families."

Nancy turned to George, who clearly had no idea what was going on. "Let's get out of here," she said.

When they'd walked down the hall a little way, George asked, "What did I miss in there?"

Nancy filled her in. "Mari wasn't kidding. I guess Midori really blew it. Everyone's incredibly mad at her."

Just then Mari came out of the sitting room and joined them. "That was awful, wasn't it?" she said dejectedly.

"Uh-huh," Nancy replied. "What did your dad mean about Midori's art school?"

"Oh, that." Mari sighed. "When she was at Senagawa, Midori kind of—well, she changed."

She paused to brush her bangs out of her eyes. "Midori was friends with some weird people, I guess. Plus, something happened between her and Ken at that time—she seemed to drift away from him. My parents finally pulled her out of the school. They said they didn't like what it was doing to her."

Nancy was thoughtful. "Were any of Midori's Senagawa friends invited to the wedding?"

"No," Mari said. "My parents would not have

them here. To tell you the truth, most of the guests are business contacts of my father's and Mr. Nakamura's."

"Can you get me the names and numbers of some of Midori's old art school friends?" Nancy persisted. "I'd like to talk to them. Maybe they'll have some idea about what's going on with Midori."

Mari nodded. "I will do it when I get home."

The three girls spent the next half hour questioning staff members of the villa—caterers, musicians, and security guards. None of them had seen Midori leave.

"She seems to have disappeared into thin air," George remarked as they walked down the hallway to Midori's dressing room.

"Of course, this place is huge," Nancy pointed out. "And so are the grounds. It's not so surprising that she managed to sneak off without being noticed."

Midori's dressing room was a Japanese-style room with a few pieces of antique furniture. An ivory-inlaid vanity table was covered with combs, brushes, mirrors, and makeup. The tatami floor was littered with bobby pins and dry cleaner's bags. The air smelled of talcum powder.

Mari nodded at a pile of clothes in the corner. "That was what Midori was wearing before she got into her kimono."

"So we know she was wearing her kimono when she left the villa," Nancy said.

"There was no way she could have gotten out of it by herself in such a short time," Mari commented.

The room opened onto a private courtyard at the side of the villa. "Come on," Nancy said.

The courtyard was bordered by tall, perfectly trimmed hedges. "Midori could have slipped out this way," Nancy observed. "This courtyard is cut off from the rest of the grounds."

"And the wedding site is at the other end of the villa," Mari added.

There was a narrow opening in the hedges, and just beyond it, a dirt path. The girls started down it. It led through a bamboo grove to one of the rear corners of the property and ended at an iron gate leading to the street.

"Look!" Nancy exclaimed.

She bent down to study something that had caught on the gate. It was a long, thickly braided cord. It had become slightly unraveled, and a few gold threads hung loose from it.

"That's Midori's *obi-jime!*" Mari cried out. Seeing the confusion on Nancy and George's faces, she added quickly, "It's part of her wedding outfit. It goes on top of the *obi,* the wide sash that holds the kimono together."

"It must have come undone when Midori went through here," Nancy said. She jiggled the gate, and it swung open.

Nancy went out into the street. There were no

cars. "Where does this street lead?" she asked Mari.

"To the left, it is a dead end," Mari replied. "And to the right, it leads through some rice fields. It connects with the highway after that."

"Midori didn't have a car with her, right?" George said. Mari nodded. "So how did she get away?"

Nancy frowned. "Good question." She tucked Midori's *obi-jime* into the pocket of her pale yellow dress and started walking back toward the villa. "Let's talk to Ken," she said.

The girls found him near the wedding site. He was sitting on a stone bench, alone, dressed in a jacket and slacks. He was watching as workers put away the folding chairs. It was after one thirty, and almost all the guests had gone home.

Nancy approached him, Mari and George at her heels.

He glanced up. "Hi," he murmured hollowly. He seemed to be in a state of shock.

Nancy sat down next to him. "I'm sorry about all this."

"You're sorry," he said bitterly. "I feel like I have been punched in the stomach."

Mari sat down on the other side of him. "Ken, Nancy is a detective," she said softly. "I have asked her to find Midori."

"We thought you might be able to give us some information about her," George piped up.

"What do you think you're doing?"

Nancy raised her eyes to see Yoko Nakamura marching toward them. Her cheeks were flushed with anger.

"My son has just suffered a terrible blow," Yoko began huffily, then fixed her blazing eyes on Mari, "thanks to your sister's childish behavior. The last thing he needs is to be reminded of her." She shook her head and muttered something in Japanese. Nancy thought it sounded like, "I always knew that Midori was no good."

Ken sighed and held up one hand. "Mother, do not make a scene. I'm fine."

"You are *not* fine," Yoko insisted firmly. "Besides, we are all ready to go." She started walking toward the villa, expecting her son to do the same.

Ken sighed again and stood up. "If you still want to talk, you can come to our house later," he said quietly to Nancy. "At five. Mari can tell you the address." Then he followed his mother inside.

"What was that all about?" George asked Mari.

"Mrs. Nakamura is angry, along with everyone else," Mari replied unhappily. "I had better go, too—my parents are probably waiting for me."

After giving Nancy and George directions to the Nakamuras' and promising to call with the names of Midori's art school friends, Mari left.

"Where to now?" George said to Nancy.

"Let's grab one of those limousines Mr.

Nakamura mentioned," Nancy suggested. "I'd like to get back to the *ryokan* and out of this dress."

"Hey, Nan," George said as they were heading for the parking lot. "I just remembered. Right before the ceremony was to start, you were pointing someone out to me—a blond guy."

Nancy stopped in her tracks. "Oh, no!" she exclaimed. "In all the excitement, I totally forgot!"

"So who was it?" George asked.

"Me by any chance?" a male voice rang out.

Nancy and George spun around. A tall guy was standing right behind them.

Nancy's heart began racing madly. It really *was* him. Golden hair, the greenest eyes she'd ever seen . . .

"Mick Devlin," she whispered.

Chapter

Four

I SPOTTED YOU a while ago, but then lost sight of you," Mick said. "Lucky that I found you again."

He stepped forward and put his hands on Nancy's shoulders. "It's good to see you," he murmured, staring into her eyes.

It was a moment before Nancy could find her voice. "It's good to see you, too," she said finally. "I thought it was you, but I couldn't believe it."

Mick smiled, then turned to George. "Hello, George," he said, kissing her on the cheek.

"Hello yourself," George said, grinning broadly. "What on earth are you doing here, Mick? Why aren't you in Australia?"

"I'm working at Nakamura Incorporated," Mick explained. "I've had an internship there for the last six months." He dug his hands into the pockets of his cream-colored linen suit. "Now it's my turn. What brings you two to Japan? Are you on a case?"

Nancy and George glanced at each other. "Well, yes," Nancy said. "But that's not why we came. The bride—well, the almost-bride—is a friend of ours."

"Talk about coincidence?" George marveled, shaking her head.

Mick winked at Nancy. "Fate always seems to bring us together, doesn't it? Remember Switzerland? And Italy?"

"And Greece," Nancy added, blushing.

Nancy, George, and Bess had spent one summer vacation traveling around Europe. They'd met Mick in Geneva, and there'd been sparks between him and Nancy from the start. He'd followed her to Rome and the Greek island of Mykonos.

In Greece Mick had proposed to her. Nancy had turned him down because she wasn't ready to settle down and because she did love Ned.

That summer, though, she and Ned had been drifting apart. That was part of the reason she'd fallen for Mick. Since then, she and Ned had patched things up, and now their relationship was as strong as ever.

"So where are you off to now?" Mick was saying.

"Back to our *ryokan*," George told him.

"Do you need a ride?" Mick asked, producing

a set of keys from his pocket. "My car's just over there—come on."

"That would be great," Nancy said, beaming. Despite the ruined wedding and Midori's disappearance, she suddenly felt inexplicably lighthearted. "Thanks, Mick."

"No problem," Mick said, then added, "Hey, here's a thought. Why don't you let me be your tour guide while you're here? Nightlife is my specialty." He put his arms around both girls' shoulders. "We can start tonight. I have passes to a fantastic rock club in Roppongi. And tomorrow night there's a *Bon Matsuri* festival at this beautiful old temple . . ."

"Penny for your thoughts," George said.

"Hmm?" Nancy turned to George, who was sitting next to her in the Nakamuras' front parlor. It was five after five, and they were waiting to talk to Ken. "I was just going over the case."

George grinned slyly. "Which case? Midori's disappearance or Mick's reappearance?"

Nancy whacked her playfully on the arm. "Oh, please. I mean, I'm really glad to run into Mick again, but that's all. I've already got a boyfriend, remember?"

"I remember," George said. "But maybe Mick doesn't have a girlfriend. He sure seemed happy to see you."

Nancy rolled her eyes, then decided to change the subject. "I've been thinking. Mrs. Kato mentioned that Midori and Ken had a date on Thursday night and that she came home early."

George nodded. "Right. She thought they might have had a fight."

"And according to both her and Mari, that's when Midori started acting strangely," Nancy went on. "I have a feeling that this fight—or whatever it was—is a major clue. Which means that Ken will be able to clear up a lot of questions for us."

George peered at her watch. "Speaking of Ken, where is he?"

"I'm sure he'll be here soon," Nancy said, then leaned back in her chair and glanced around the room.

The parlor was an eclectic blend of Asian, American, and European decor. The leather couch was framed by a pair of red lacquer end tables from China. The walls were covered with Japanese woodblock prints, English still-life paintings, and old photographs of New York City.

"This place is amazing," Nancy declared.

"The Nakamuras must be loaded," George added.

Just then the door swung open, and Ken strode in. "I'm sorry to keep you waiting," he said, then sat down in a chair opposite the girls. "Have you heard from Midori yet?" Nancy couldn't help notice the eager spark in his eyes.

"Not yet," Nancy replied. "Have you?"

The eager spark faded. "No," Ken said slowly. "I do not expect to, either. Although I was hoping . . ." He paused and sighed. "Actually, I don't know what I was hoping."

"Mari asked me to find Midori," Nancy reminded him.

"I don't know why you're even bothering," Ken muttered. He sounded angry now. "I mean, Midori obviously wants to be as far away from me as possible. Although it would have been nice if she had broken things off before our wedding day, don't you think?"

Nancy was about to point out that Midori might have run away for a reason having nothing to do with Ken. But she could see that he was speaking more from wounded pride than logic, so she decided not to say anything.

"Did you have any idea she was going to disappear?" George asked him.

Ken turned away for a second. There was bitterness in his voice as he said, "She could not have surprised me more if she had set fire to the place. She never gave me any indication that she was having second thoughts."

"How about Thursday night?" Nancy prompted. "Mrs. Kato told us that you had a date with her. But Midori went home early, right?"

"Right. That was odd, actually." Ken picked up a bronze statuette from the coffee table and began toying with it absentmindedly.

"Midori came to my office around five," he continued. "I was in a meeting, so I asked her to wait in the conference room until I was through. When I went to get her twenty minutes later, she wasn't there. She'd left word with the receptionist that she wasn't feeling well and had to go home."

"What was wrong with her?" Nancy asked.

"I have no idea," Ken replied. "I called her, but her mother told me she was resting and couldn't come to the phone. I tried calling her again yesterday, but once again I was told the same story. Then today was the wedding." He gave a sad shrug.

Nancy took a deep breath, then said, "Ken, I know this is really personal. But I need to ask— were you and Midori getting along all right?"

Ken stared at her, his dark eyes flashing. "Midori and I *had* an excellent relationship," he declared firmly. Then he added, "Do not misunderstand me. We have had our problems. Like when she was at Senagawa. But that was a while ago."

Nancy's ears perked up. "You mean Senagawa Art College? Mari said her sister changed while she was there."

"She did," Ken said grimly. "Midori found a bunch of new friends, and suddenly she had no

36

time for me. There was a jerk she was running around with there, too."

Another guy? Nancy wanted to ask, but before she had a chance, Ken cleared his throat and said, "I do not want to discuss it. Anyway, her parents pulled her out, and we patched up our relationship."

Just then Connor entered the room. "Ken, your uncle—" He stopped. "Oh, I'm sorry, I didn't realize you had company. Anyway, your uncle needs to see you right away. It's important, he said."

Nancy noticed that Connor didn't bother to greet either her or George. Nice guy, she thought.

"I'd better see what he wants," Ken said to the girls, standing up. "If you have any more questions, feel free to call me here or at the office. Here's my card." He fished one out of his wallet and handed it to Nancy.

Connor gave Nancy a brief, curious glance, then left the room. Ken started to follow him, then turned and said quietly, "Please call me if you hear from Midori—day or night."

After promising to do so, Nancy and George headed for the front door. As George reached for her leather sandals, she said, "What do you think?"

"I think we should go back to the *ryokan* and wait for Mari's call," Nancy replied. "After talking to Ken, I'm more anxious than ever to get that list of Senagawa names."

"That business about Thursday night—" George began, then stopped. Ken's mother was marching down the hallway toward them. She was dressed in an ivory silk pantsuit with several gold chains dangling from her neck.

She stopped and fixed her eyes on Nancy. "I see you have been visiting my son," she said coolly. "Are you conducting an investigation into Midori's disappearance?"

"Yes," Nancy replied. "Why? Do you have some information for us, Mrs. Nakamura?"

"Information?" Yoko drew her red lips into a thin, angry line. "The only information I have for you is this. You will stop your search for Midori immediately—or you will have to answer to me!"

Chapter

Five

W HAT?" George cried out.

"Let me get this straight," Nancy said slowly. "You don't *want* me to find your son's fiancée?"

"As far as I am concerned, Midori ceased to be Ken's fiancée as of this morning," Yoko declared firmly. "You are Americans—you do not understand the seriousness of what she has done. When two families settle on a marriage arrangement for their children, it is a sacred contract, to be honored at all costs."

"But what if Midori had a good reason not to go through with the wedding?" Nancy suggested.

"There is *no* reason to excuse her actions," Yoko scoffed. "Midori has dishonored and embarrassed the Katos and the Nakamuras. If you continue with your investigation, it will only make things worse for all of us."

Nancy studied her curiously. Some instinct told her that Yoko wasn't being completely open, but Nancy knew better than to push things.

"We'll think about what you said," Nancy replied smoothly. "Now, if you'll excuse us." She glanced at George, and they turned to go.

Yoko managed to get in one last warning. "Forget Midori Kato," she said, her voice cold as steel. "Or you will be most sorry."

Back at the *ryokan*, Nancy and George found a message from Mari. Nancy returned her call while George tuned in to a baseball game on the television set.

"I found only one Senagawa name for you," Mari said to Nancy after exchanging hellos. "Hana Endo—she works at a boutique called Explosion in the Harajuku district. I don't have her home number, but this is her work number." She rattled it off, and Nancy took it down.

"I am sorry I don't have more names," Mari went on. "I searched all through Midori's desk. She usually carries her address book in her purse, and I assume she has that with her."

"How did you get Hana's number, then?" Nancy asked.

"I came across an old flyer for a performance piece Hana did at the school. It had her workplace and number scribbled on it."

Nancy considered this, then said, "Midori

never talked about her Senagawa friends with you?"

"No," Mari responded. "As I said before, she went through a weird phase there. She kept things from our parents—and from me." Nancy heard the hurt in the girl's voice.

"Do you know if Midori dated anyone there?" Nancy pressed.

"At Senagawa?" Mari paused. "Not that I know of."

Nancy then told Mari about their encounter with Yoko Nakamura. When she'd finished, Mari said, "Mrs. Nakamura actually *ordered* you to drop the investigation?"

"Yes," Nancy replied. "Can you think why she'd do that, Mari? Aside from the reasons she gave, that is?"

Mari was silent for a moment. "Midori mentioned to me once that Mrs. Nakamura did not like her much," she said finally.

Nancy's ears perked up. "Oh, really? And why did your sister think that?"

"Midori figured that Mrs. Nakamura had a different sort of girl in mind for Ken," Mari explained. "Maybe the daughter of one of her country club friends. We are not exactly poor, but the Nakamuras—well, they live in a mansion. They party with politicians and celebrities."

"So why did Mrs. Nakamura agree to an

arranged marriage between Midori and Ken?" Nancy asked.

"The match was decided a long time ago by my father and Ken's father, when he was still alive," Mari replied. "They were old friends. Mrs. Nakamura had no say in the matter."

"Why not?" Nancy said.

"It is just the way things are in Japan. Men always make the big decisions. Wives get no vote."

"So even though Mrs. Nakamura didn't approve of Midori, she had to go along with what her husband wanted," Nancy said slowly. "No wonder she wants me to drop this investigation. I'm sure she'd be totally thrilled if Ken never saw Midori again."

Then she sat up, her blue eyes flashing keenly. "What if Mrs. Nakamura is responsible for Midori's disappearance? She couldn't openly oppose the marriage arrangement, right? So maybe she decided to keep the wedding from happening. Maybe it's possible she said something to Midori to upset her and make her run away."

"Like what?" Mari said.

"I'm not sure," Nancy murmured. "Mrs. Nakamura seems like the sort of person who always goes after what she wants. It wouldn't surprise me one bit if she took it upon herself to sabotage Ken and Midori's wedding."

The girls talked a little longer. Nancy promised

to keep Mari informed about what her investigation turned up.

As soon as the conversation ended, she tried calling Hana Endo at Explosion, but a recording told her that the store wouldn't be open until noon on Sunday.

"So how do we find out if your theory about Yoko Nakamura is right?" George asked once Nancy had hung up.

"Any ideas?" Nancy said, stretching her long, slender legs across the tatami floor.

"One way to do it would be to accuse her outright," George suggested. "Mrs. Nakamura seems kind of hotheaded. If she's guilty, she might accidentally give herself away."

Nancy considered this, then said, "She's too smart for that. Besides, even if we managed to prove that she scared Midori away, we still don't know where Midori is now."

"Good point," George agreed.

"Assuming that she wanted to lie low for a while," Nancy went on, "she might have gone to a hotel or a *ryokan* someplace. Or she could be staying with friends." She added, "Which reminds me—"

"Hmm?"

"Tomorrow morning I'd like to go by the Katos' house to search Midori's room," Nancy said. "We might be able to find a clue. And after that we'll head over to Explosion and talk to Hana."

"Sounds like a good plan." George glanced at her watch. "Hey, we'd better get a move on if we're going to meet Mick at that rock club. We have to change, grab some dinner—"

"Good idea," Nancy said. "I noticed a *yakitori* place around the corner."

"Yakitori?" George asked warily. "I was thinking more along the lines of a cheeseburger."

There was a knock on the sliding door. "I'll get that," Nancy said, rising.

She opened the door, but there was no one there. Instead Nancy found a tray of covered dishes lying on the floor of the hallway. On it was a white card with a hand-scripted message that read: "Compliments of the Sakura Ryokan."

"What great timing," Nancy said, carrying the tray into the room and setting it down on the lacquer table. "Wasn't it sweet of Mrs. Ito?"

George sighed. "I guess this means the cheeseburger's out."

They sat down at the table. "I don't know what to try first," Nancy said, uncovering some of the dishes. "Maybe I'll start with this one." She pointed at a spiny fish that had been artfully arranged on a green glazed platter.

George made a face. "It's raw, isn't it?"

Nancy grinned and picked up a piece of the fish with her chopsticks.

"Is there anything *cooked* on this tray?" George grumbled.

There was another knock on the sliding door.

This time George got up to answer it. It was a young maid with fresh towels and two *yukata,* kimono-style cotton robes. She entered, bowed, then headed for the bathroom to drop off her load.

"Thank you," Nancy called out, then turned back to her dinner. "You should try this, George. See, you dip the raw fish in this bowl of soy sauce and wasabi mustard—"

That was as far as she got. The maid, who was passing behind Nancy, froze in her tracks and dropped her towels and *yukata.* Then, before Nancy could react, the young woman shouted something incoherent and grabbed Nancy's arm.

Chapter

Six

Nancy's chopsticks dropped to the floor.

"What are you doing!" she cried out. Out of the corner of her eye, she could see George getting up to intervene.

It was unnecessary because the maid suddenly let go of Nancy's arm and began apologizing profusely.

"I am deeply sorry," she murmured in stilted English, bowing over and over again. "I did not mean to frighten you."

Nancy straightened up and ran a hand through her hair. She glanced at the maid, then up at George, who was hovering over them with an expression of total confusion on her face.

Nancy took a deep breath and turned back to the maid. "What was that all about?" she asked sharply.

The maid bowed again, then said, "I was trying to prevent you from eating that." She indicated the piece of raw fish that Nancy had just dipped into the soy sauce and wasabi mixture. It was lying on the floor, along with Nancy's chopsticks.

Nancy frowned. "I don't understand. Why shouldn't I eat that fish?"

"That is no ordinary fish," the maid explained. "That is fugu, or blowfish—a great Japanese delicacy. The fugu has several poisonous organs, which must be removed by a special chef. Anyone who even tastes improperly prepared fugu suffocates and dies within half an hour."

"What!" George exclaimed.

The maid pointed to the white "Compliments of Sakura Ryokan" card lying on the tray. "I saw that as I passed behind you," she told Nancy. "At the same time I saw the fugu. I knew something was wrong. We do not serve fugu in our kitchen."

Nancy's eyes widened.

"Perhaps I overreacted," the maid went on, blushing. "But when I realized that you were about to put the fugu in your mouth, I did not want you to take a chance."

Nancy shook her head and put her hand on the young woman's arm. "No, you didn't overreact. You may have saved my life."

The maid's instincts were right. When Mrs. Ito came up to their room to discuss the matter, the manager quickly confirmed that the Sakura

Ryokan did not serve fugu. She also explained that the tray of food was not from their kitchen.

"We do not offer complimentary dinners to our guests," Mrs. Ito stated. "Just breakfast and tea in the afternoons."

"Do you have any idea where this tray came from?" Nancy asked.

Mrs. Ito nodded. "About twenty minutes ago, I let a delivery boy in to take this food to you. He said you had phoned the restaurant to order it. Our guests often order food, so I did not think anything of it."

"Which restaurant was he from?" George asked.

"I did not notice," Mrs. Ito replied, bristling slightly. "The boy was unfamiliar to me, but I had no reason to be suspicious of him."

"What did he look like?" Nancy said.

Mrs. Ito shrugged. "He had a crew cut. That is all I remember."

Nancy nodded, then pointed at the fugu. "Mrs. Ito, can you tell if this has poison in it?"

"Of course," she said. "My father was a fugu chef."

She peered at the spiky fish closely. Then she poked at it with a pair of chopsticks.

After a moment of inspecting it, she gasped. "This fugu is full of poison!" she announced.

Nancy paled slightly, thinking of how close she'd come to taking a bite. "How do you know?"

"The liver has not been removed, and it is one of the most toxic parts of the fish!" Mrs. Ito said. "I am most distressed. Who would do such a terrible thing?"

Nancy didn't reply, although Yoko Nakamura's name came immediately to mind. Would Ken's mother have resorted to murder to keep Nancy from tracking down Midori? she asked herself.

Nancy and George were twenty minutes late meeting Mick. He was waiting for them on a bustling street corner, in front of a small building with no sign or windows.

"Hi," Mick said, waving. He was dressed in jeans, a white T-shirt, and black linen jacket. "I was starting to wonder if you had been kidnapped . . ." His words trailed off when he saw the expressions on the girls' faces. "What's wrong?"

Nancy watched a group of Japanese teens enter the building and said, "It's kind of a long story. Let's go inside, and we'll fill you in."

Just inside the entrance a doorman took Mick's passes. He was wearing a black vintage tuxedo and yellow baseball cap. "Welcome to Puppy Love Live," he said to them.

"Puppy Love Live?" George repeated, glancing at Mick. "What does that mean?"

Mick smiled and shrugged. "Who knows? The

Japanese are great at coming up with weird names for things."

The interior of the club was part Gothic, part Arabian fantasy. The cavernous space was split into individual rooms, separated by wispy chiffon curtains that hung from the ceiling. Each room was furnished with velvet and satin settees in brilliant golds, purples, and reds. The air was sweet with the smell of patchouli incense.

In the center was a large dance floor, lit from above by an enormous antique chandelier. At the moment the floor was mobbed with teens dancing to a British rock tune.

A young girl passed by Nancy and her friends carrying a basket of daisies. She gave one to each of them, then moved on.

"What a fun place," George remarked, tucking her daisy into the pocket of her black silk shirt.

"Isn't it?" Mick said. "I asked a friend from work to meet us. I think I see him sitting over there."

Nancy and George followed Mick to one of the chiffon-shrouded rooms. A short guy with curly brown hair and glasses rose to greet them. He wore jeans and a T-shirt that said: "I'd Rather Be on Star System 434-CL."

"Greetings," he said, giving the girls a nervous little wave. "Gil Armstrong, at your service."

"Gil's a fellow Aussie and Nakamura intern," Mick explained, then introduced Nancy and

George to him. "Let's all get comfortable, shall we?"

He put his hand on Nancy's elbow and pulled her down on a velvet settee. That left George to sit with Gil, across from them.

"Mick tells me you're an athlete, George," Gil said, flashing her a toothy grin.

George threw Nancy a helpless look, as if to say, "Is this guy supposed to be my date?" Then she turned to Gil and said, "Um, sure, I guess you could call me that."

While the two of them were talking, Mick moved closer to Nancy and said, "Is this a good time to tell me what happened to you earlier tonight?"

Nancy nodded, then filled him in on the case. She ended with an account of the near deadly fugu incident.

"On our way down here, George and I checked out all the restaurants in our neighborhood," Nancy finished. "It was a real dead end. None of them serves fugu, and none of them could identify our delivery guy."

Mick frowned. "Somebody really wants you out of the picture—permanently," he said, concerned. "Do you think it's Yoko Nakamura?"

"I don't know," Nancy admitted. "She's the only suspect I've got. But it's really hard for me to believe she'd kill me to keep Ken and Midori apart." She paused, then said, "My instincts tell me there's more to Midori's disappearance than we thought—something major enough to make someone want to kill me. I just have to figure out what it is and who's responsible."

Mick leaned forward and touched her cheek lightly. "Well, you know you can count on me," he murmured. "I'll do anything to help."

"Thanks, Mick," Nancy said. His touch made her feel awkward. "Hey, why don't we dance?" she suggested.

"Sure," Mick said, standing up. "Gil? George? You want to join us?"

"I'm really not much of a dancer," Gil replied quickly. "Besides, George and I are having a great talk about Japanese politics."

George's eyes widened skeptically at this remark.

Nancy followed Mick through the chiffon curtains. "I hope George is having a good time," she whispered.

"Oh, sure," Mick whispered back. "She and Gil seem to be getting along fine."

The dance floor was still packed, and Nancy and Mick were pushed together as they tried to move to the music.

"Popular place," Nancy remarked, raising her arms to let two dancers pass.

A moment later the music shifted to a slow number. Mick held out his hand to Nancy. "I'm game if you are," he said.

She smiled and took his hand. "Sure."

A second later they were holding each other and swaying slowly. "Will you be mad if I tell you that this reminds me of old times?" Mick whispered in her ear.

Nancy felt her breath catch in her throat. "No," she whispered back. She hated to admit it, but it was comfortable being in his arms again. She felt herself moving imperceptibly closer to him.

Just then a warning light went off in her head. She stepped back and shook her head.

"What's wrong?" Mick murmured.

Nancy looked up at him. "Listen, Mick," she said seriously. "You know I'm with Ned now. I can't be more than friends with any other guy."

Mick was silent for a moment, then said, "I understand, Nancy. If you just want to be friends, that's fine with me." He grinned. "On two conditions. I get you for the rest of this dance and you go to the festival with me tomorrow night."

Nancy laughed softly. "You drive a hard bargain, Mick Devlin."

Without any further words Mick took her in his arms and they began dancing again. Nancy closed her eyes and put her head against his chest. As the slow, romantic song played on, she willed herself to enjoy the moment and not think about the past or the future. Or Ned.

* * *

"You went to Puppy Love Live last night?" Mari said. "I'm so jealous. Isn't it great?"

She, Nancy, and George were sitting in the Katos' backyard enjoying the morning sun. From inside the house, Nancy could hear the sounds of Toshiko Kato chopping vegetables. Her husband was in the front yard trimming the hedges.

"We had a terrific time," George replied. "And we really needed it, too, especially after—" She hesitated and glanced at Nancy.

Mari stared at George, then at Nancy. "What?" she said anxiously.

Nancy took a deep breath and told her about the fugu. By the time she'd finished, Mari was paler.

"I don't get it," Mari murmured. "You don't think it had anything to do with Midori, do you?"

"It has to," Nancy replied gravely. "And until we figure out who's behind it, we'll all have to keep our eyes open and be very careful."

Just then Nancy spotted a flash of white behind a jasmine bush. "What was that?" she asked, pointing.

Mari walked over to the bush and came back a second later with a huge cat in her arms. It was all white except for a few black and red spots, and had a small stub for a tail.

"This is Kunta," Mari explained. "He's a *mi-ke,* which means 'three colors.' He usually lives in Midori's room—he's kind of her cat. He really misses her."

At the mention of Midori's name, Kunta let out a loud, pathetic howl.

George stroked him under the chin. "Poor Kunta," she cooed.

Mari set Kunta down and brushed her hands together. Bits of cat fur fluttered through the air. "Speaking of Midori's room, Nancy—you said that you wanted to go through it, right? You want to do it now?"

"Sure," Nancy said, standing up.

The three girls made their way upstairs. Kunta followed, rubbing against their legs and purring as he went.

"He's a sweetie, isn't he?" Mari called over her shoulder as they entered Midori's room. "My sister found him in the street five years ago and—"

She stopped abruptly and gasped.

Nancy, who was right behind her, looked around quickly. Midori's room was a mess. There were papers and books scattered all over the peach-colored carpet. A chair had been knocked over.

"Her room didn't look like this last night," Mari said in a low voice. "It was neat."

"Are you saying—" Nancy began.

Mari turned to Nancy, her eyes wide. "I think someone's been in here."

Chapter

Seven

Y OU MEAN, like a burglar?" George said incredulously. "But what could anyone have wanted in here?"

"Mari, is anything missing?" Nancy said quickly.

"I'm not sure," Mari replied. "But I'll check."

"Try not to touch anything if you can," Nancy told her gently. "If we have to call in the police, they'll probably want to dust for fingerprints."

Mari nodded and began circling the room. Her eyes swept over Midori's bookshelves, dresser, and vanity table. While she did this, Nancy glanced around. The room was very Midori. Art posters covered almost every inch of the walls, and there was an easel in one corner with a half-finished pastel drawing.

"All her good jewelry's in the safe downstairs," Mari told Nancy and George. "And I know she keeps whatever money she has in her purse."

Mari continued to circle the room. Then she stopped at Midori's desk.

"Her diary," she said suddenly.

"What?" Nancy said.

"Midori's diary," Mari said urgently. "It was on top of her desk last night—right there."

"What does it look like?" George asked.

"It's about this big," Mari said, holding up her hands to indicate a book about four by six inches. "And it has a light purple cover with a flimsy gold lock. I am not sure where Midori keeps the key."

"What on earth would anyone want with her diary?" George said, frowning.

"I don't know," Nancy admitted. She went over to the window and noted that it was locked from the inside. "Listen, Mari. Before we go any further, let's get your parents up here to make sure they didn't take the diary."

The Katos were as surprised as Mari had been by the state of Midori's room.

"Neither one of us has been in here since yesterday morning," Toshiko said, wringing her hands.

"That settles it, then," Nancy said firmly. "We should call the police."

Tadashi shook his head vehemently. "No police," he said. "I'm sure this is Midori's doing.

57

She's always been absurdly devoted to that diary. She probably came to the house in the middle of the night and sneaked into her room to get it. Of course, she was too ashamed to face us."

"Midori wouldn't have come home and not told us, Tadashi," Toshiko insisted. "We are her family."

"After what Midori did yesterday, nothing she does should surprise us," Tadashi retorted.

"You honestly think *Midori* took the diary, Mr. Kato?" Nancy asked, puzzled.

Tadashi shrugged. "Why not? Nothing else in the house is missing. I myself opened the family safe not an hour ago, and everything was fine."

"Maybe you're right, Tadashi," his wife said slowly. "After all, we have bolt locks on both the front and back doors. How could anyone get in without a key?"

Nancy thought about her own lockpicking kit, which she always carried with her, but didn't say anything. She made a mental note to check both locks.

"But what about this mess?" George asked Tadashi, waving her hand at the books and papers strewn all over the floor. "Midori would have known where her diary was—she wouldn't have needed to rifle through her stuff."

"Maybe she could not find her way in the dark," Tadashi suggested. "To be perfectly frank, until Midori apologizes, what she does or doesn't do is of no concern to me." He turned and walked out of the room.

"Tadashi!" his wife cried out, following him.

Mari stared dejectedly at Nancy and George.

Nancy laid a hand on her arm. "It's okay, Mari. We'll find your sister."

George nodded encouragingly.

Nancy walked over to Midori's desk and gazed at it thoughtfully. "The trouble is, we've only got a few things to go on," she said. "The gold cord from Midori's kimono, Yoko Nakamura telling us to drop the case, the fugu delivered by a guy with a crew cut—and now the missing diary."

"So what's our next move, Nan?" George asked, plopping down on Midori's bed.

"Let's finish searching here for clues and check the front and back doors." Nancy suggested.

Nancy and George ran into the subway car a split second before the doors slammed shut.

"Whew, that was close," Nancy said. She glanced around the crowded car. "There are two seats over there."

They sat down next to two guys. One of them gave the girls an appraising look, then began speaking to his companion in a low voice.

"I think we're being checked out," George whispered to Nancy.

"I don't know about you, but I don't need any more men in my life," Nancy joked.

George frowned. "Speaking of too many men, is Mick bringing that Gil person along to the festival tonight?"

Nancy studied George with concern. "Is he that bad?"

"No, he's not *that* bad," George replied dryly. "If you like geeky guys who talk your ear off about stuff like superconductors and the role of the Japanese art market in illegal political contributions." She broke into a grin. "Hey, don't sweat it, Nan. You've got enough to worry about, with the case and everything.

"Oh, right—the case," Nancy said, sighing. "To tell you the truth, this diary thing has me stumped. And searching Midori's room turned up zero."

"It's weird, isn't it?" George said. "We inspected all the doors and windows at the Katos', and none of them had been tampered with. So how did the thief get in?"

"And what did he or she want with Midori's diary?" Nancy added. "Did Midori write something in it that someone wanted to find out about?" She shook her head. "I'm beginning to wonder if Mr. Kato is right. Maybe Midori *did* come back and take it."

"If you ask me, Mr. Kato's too mad at Midori to think straight," George remarked, leaning back in her seat. "I mean, you'd think he'd be more worried than angry, wouldn't you?"

"The Japanese expect a lot from their children," Nancy mused. "And being shamed and dishonored in public—they take it pretty seriously."

Two stops later, Nancy and George got off the subway and headed for Takeshita-doori, the main strip in the Harajuku district. It was a narrow street crammed with inexpensive-looking boutiques and restaurants. It was mobbed with leather- and denim-clad Japanese teens. Rock music blasted from outdoor speakers, adding to the mood of chaos and excitement.

"This is wild," George declared.

"Definitely," Nancy said. "If we weren't so busy with this case, I'd love to check out some of these stores." She paused and looked around. "I don't see Explosion, do you?"

"No," George replied, stepping aside to avoid bumping into a guy with blue spiked hair.

As they walked, Nancy said, "I hope this Hana Endo lead pays off. The more I think about it, the more Midori's disappearance seems linked to her time at Senagawa Art College. All the business about her changing, keeping secrets from her family, drifting away from Ken—it's pretty suspicious."

She halted suddenly and pointed at a neon green building. "Hey, there's Explosion. Come on, George."

Nancy and George blinked as they went

through the door. The inside of the store was almost pitch-black, except for the high-tech track lights that illuminated the racks of clothing. A synthesizer piece that sounded like clanking machinery was playing in the background.

Nancy proceeded to wander around the store, stopping occasionally to look at the clothes. Most of it was black and made of unusual fabrics—vinyl, plastic, rubber, fake fur. Along the way she passed several customers, but no salesclerks.

Then she almost bumped into a girl holding an armful of fringed black miniskirts. She had very short hair and was chewing gum loudly. She wore a skeleton earring in one ear and a silver H in the other. This could be Hana, Nancy thought excitedly.

"Hi," she said. "Do you work here?"

"Yeah," the girl replied in a bored voice. "You want to try something on?"

Nancy looked at the miniskirts. "One of those," she said quickly. "I'm not sure about Japanese sizes. What do you think I'd wear?"

The girl sorted through the bundle in her arms and handed Nancy two skirts. "Try these," she said. "You know where the dressing room is?"

"I've never been here before," Nancy said, then added, "A friend of mine told me to come here—Midori Kato. She said it was a great store."

"You know Midori?" the girl repeated, sounding interested.

Bingo, Nancy thought. "You know her, too?" she said innocently.

"We went to Senagawa together for a while," the girl explained.

George came up to them. "Hi," she said uncertainly, her eyes moving from Nancy to the girl and back to Nancy again.

"This is my friend George," Nancy explained. "I'm Nancy. And you're—"

"Hana," the girl replied. "If you see Midori, tell her I said hi. I haven't seen her in a while." She pursed her lips, blew a bubble, and popped it before adding, "Not since her totally uptight parents pulled her out of school."

"Really?" Nancy said. "Actually, I haven't seen her in a while, either. I was hoping to run into her."

Hana shrugged. "You might try Café Vertigo —she used to hang out there a lot. But I doubt she'll be there."

Nancy remembered the miniskirts she was holding. "I'm starving all of a sudden. Maybe George and I will head over to Café Vertigo, then come back to try these on."

Hana took them from her. "Suit yourself."

After thanking her, Nancy and George headed for the café, which was just around the corner. It was a small, dark, cavelike place with colorful murals on the walls. There were a dozen teens sitting around a few mismatched tables and drinking tiny cups of very black, bitter-smelling coffee. Most of them were wearing ripped denim shorts, torn T-shirts, and combat boots.

"I get the feeling we don't fit in here," George whispered. "Our clothes have no holes in them."

"I know what you mean," Nancy whispered back. Then she noticed three teens—two girls and a guy—sitting in the corner. The guy was wearing a Senagawa Art College T-shirt like Midori's.

Nancy approached the table. The three teens stopped talking and looked up at her. "You lost?" the guy asked coldly in excellent, unaccented English.

Nancy forced herself to smile. "Sorry, my mistake." She nodded at one of the girls. "I thought you were Midori Kato. I guess I was wrong."

"Midori!" the girl exclaimed. "She no longer comes in here."

Nancy watched the three carefully. None of them was reacting suspiciously to Midori's name —they merely seemed curious.

George walked up to the table holding two cups of espresso. "Here," she said, handing one to Nancy.

Nancy took the cup. "I was wrong," she told George meaningfully. "I thought this girl was my friend Midori, but she's not."

"Oh!" George pretended to study the girl's face. "She's definitely not."

"Midori's probably off getting married to her rich Prince Charming by now," the guy muttered.

"Ken Naka-something," the second girl spoke up. "I ran into him and Midori once. He is very handsome."

"Yumiko, you have no taste," the other girl said scornfully. "He is nothing but expensive clothes."

The girl named Yumiko shrugged. "Midori told me he writes poetry. I think that is romantic."

Remembering what Ken had said about Midori running around with a guy while she was at art school, Nancy decided to take a stab in the dark. "I don't think I've ever met Ken. Is he the guy she used to hang out with at Senagawa?"

The three teens stared at one another, then broke into laughter. "You're kidding, right?" the guy said. "Mad Dog Hayashi and Midori's zillionaire boyfriend aren't even from the same galaxy."

Nancy tried to hide her excitement. She was finally getting somewhere! "Mad Dog Hayashi?" she repeated nonchalantly, taking a sip of her espresso. "Who's he?"

"A third-year at Senagawa—a painter," Yumiko explained. "His studio is just across Yoyogi Park. A red building near the Mikado Restaurant. It used to be a slaughterhouse."

"It wasn't really a slaughterhouse," the other girl said in exasperation. "Mad Dog just likes to tell people that."

"Um, is Mad Dog his real name?" George piped up.

"No," the girl replied. "He gave himself that nickname from some American comic book character—a warrior who rides a motorcycle all across the planet Volcanitron."

George turned to Nancy and made a face. "Sounds like a real fun guy," she said in a low voice.

"Uh-huh," Nancy replied vaguely. She was eager to get out of there and pay Mad Dog a visit. It was beginning to look as if he and Midori had been an item at some point. And if that were true, he might be a useful source of information.

She put her cup down on a nearby table and grinned at the three teens. "We've got to run. Sorry again about the mistake."

Nancy and George found Yoyogi Park easily, but had a hard time getting through it. It was crammed with teens dancing to American rock songs from the fifties.

"That was pretty brilliant how you got Mad Dog Hayashi's name," George said, squeezing past a guy doing the twist.

"Thanks," Nancy replied. "I wish I'd been a little more brilliant about getting his address, though. It might be tough finding his place."

When they'd gotten across Yoyogi Park, Nancy stopped a police officer on the street and asked for directions to the Mikado Restaurant.

"He said seven blocks this way," Nancy translated for George. "Come on."

The neighborhood became desolate as the girls walked. There were fewer stores and restaurants, and more run-down warehouses and vacant lots.

Nancy pointed at a small wooden building with a faded yellow sign. "'The Mikado Restaurant,'" she read out loud.

A few minutes later they found themselves standing in a dirt lot surrounded by a sagging wire fence. At the far end of it was a two-story red warehouse with graffiti sprayed all over it. A skinny black cat was sitting on a windowsill, staring suspiciously at the girls.

"Is this the right place?" George said apprehensively. "It's kind of depressing. Maybe we should go home and just call the guy."

"Oh, come on, George, where's your spirit of adventure?" Nancy teased, taking her by the arm. "It'll be fun meeting this Mad Dog person. Plus, he may be able to help us find Midori."

Just outside the security door, there were two buzzers labeled in Japanese. "There are two studios in this building," Nancy noted. "Probably one upstairs and one downstairs." She squinted at the Japanese characters on the labels. "I think the top one says 'Hayashi,' but I'm not sure."

Nancy pressed both buzzers, just in case, then waited. Nothing happened.

The black cat, who was still sitting on the windowsill, hissed ferociously at the girls.

"Nice kitty," George said weakly. "Hey, Nan, let's go. No one's home."

"In a minute," Nancy said. She jiggled the doorknob. Locked.

She reached into her purse and pulled a credit card out of her wallet. "I just want to look around a little bit," she explained to George. "Then we'll go, okay?"

George glanced around. "I don't know, Nan," she said doubtfully.

Nancy bent down and slipped the credit card into the crack of the door. "This lock's kind of tricky," she murmured, jiggling the card. "But I think I can feel it giving—"

Just then, Nancy heard a loud rumbling noise.

She turned in time to see an enormous motorcycle tearing around the corner of the building. Its driver was a well-built guy dressed in ripped-up jeans, a black T-shirt, and a studded leather vest and wristbands. A large helmet covered his head, obscuring his face.

Nancy realized that he was heading straight for her and George—and he wasn't slowing down!

Chapter

Eight

GET AGAINST THE WALL!" Nancy cried out to George. Then she slipped her credit card back into her purse and flattened herself against the front of the building.

The motorcycle screeched to a halt a few feet from them, kicking up a cloud of dust and gravel. The black cat hissed, leaped off its perch, and ran off.

The driver cut the ignition and climbed off the bike.

"You almost hit us," Nancy said sharply. "Didn't you see us?"

The guy removed his helmet. He was young—in his early twenties, Nancy thought—and handsome in a rugged sort of way. He had a reddish black crew cut, and he wore a tiny gold stud in each ear. He looked as though he hadn't shaved in a few days.

"I saw you all right," the guy muttered angrily. "You were trying to break into my building."

Uh-oh, Nancy thought. Then she got an idea. "This is all your fault," she said huffily to George.

George, who'd been eyeing the guy anxiously, turned to stare at Nancy.

"My friend and I came by to see an artist named Mad Cat Hayashi," Nancy explained to the biker. "He wasn't here, so we decided to wait for him. We got bored, so Jane, here, offered to teach me some of her tricks." She smiled sweetly. "And I thought credit cards were only good for shopping!"

The guy glared at her. "You expect me to buy that story?"

"Story?" Nancy echoed. "Come on, do we look like thieves? We really are here to see Mad Cat Hayashi."

The guy tucked his helmet under one arm and frowned. "Mad *Dog* Hayashi. Get the name right."

Nancy grinned at George. "Hey, we found him—isn't that great?"

"Yeah, great," George grumbled.

Nancy threw her a warning look.

"I mean, *great!*" George repeated, smiling nervously.

"Our friend Midori Kato recommended you,"

Nancy told Mad Dog, watching him closely. "She said we had to buy some of your art before you got too famous."

At the mention of Midori's name, Nancy thought she saw a flicker of something in Mad Dog's expression. Was it fear? It was gone in a flash, and Nancy wondered if she had imagined it.

Mad Dog suddenly moved toward Nancy, his jaw clenched and his eyes glittering fiercely.

"You," he growled. "You're not here to buy art. You're here to cause trouble." He grabbed Nancy's arm roughly. "If I ever catch you around here again, I'll break both your legs—and your friend's, too. Do we understand each other?"

Without waiting for a reply, he turned and went inside, slamming the door behind him. A moment later Nancy heard him stomping up some stairs.

She rubbed her arm gingerly. "He's got some grip."

"What's his *problem?*" George said shakily.

"I wish I knew," Nancy replied. "My guess is that he's hiding something about Midori. Two seconds after I brought up her name, he was threatening us."

George tugged on Nancy's arm. "Can we please get out of here before he comes back? I don't know about you, but I like my legs the way they are."

"Sure," Nancy said. "We'd better get back to the *ryokan* and change for the festival, anyway."

It was almost dark by the time Nancy and George reached the temple where the Bon Matsuri festival was to take place.

"Mick and Gil are meeting us at the gate around the corner," Nancy said, pointing.

"It's hard to move too fast in this getup," George complained, indicating her cotton *yukata* robe. "Are you sure we're supposed to be dressed like this? I mean, this is what the maid at the *ryokan* gives us to put on after our baths!"

"Mick told me that it's *the* thing to wear at these festivals," Nancy replied merrily. "Hey—I think I see them."

Mick and Gil were leaning against an iron gate. They, too, were wearing *yukata.*

Mick came up to Nancy and kissed her on the cheek. "Hi, gorgeous."

As casual as it was, the kiss sent a tingle down Nancy's spine. Mick still had that effect on her.

"Hi, Mick," she said after a moment, trying to steady her voice.

"I was just teaching Mick the names of the more obscure constellations," Gil spoke up, then turned to George. "It's nice to see you again. I've been looking forward to continuing our discussion about politics."

George shot Nancy a helpless look as Gil took her elbow and steered her inside the gates.

Mick reached for Nancy's hand. "So we don't get separated," he explained, his green eyes twinkling. "It's pretty crowded in there."

Nancy thought about objecting, then changed her mind.

Inside the gate, the temple grounds were magical. There were white paper lanterns strung up everywhere, and the trees and bushes twinkled with fireflies. Couples strolled arm in arm, sharing big pink puffs of cotton candy. In the distance Nancy could hear a band playing a haunting Japanese melody.

The four of them paused to watch several children who were bent over a brook, floating small boats made of straw. "That's cute, isn't it?" Nancy remarked.

"It's part of the Bon Matsuri tradition," Gil said, pushing his glasses up his nose. "You see, this festival is also called the 'Festival of the Dead.' The purpose of it is to welcome back the spirits of one's dead ancestors." He pointed to the boats. "At the end of the festival, the spirits are sent back to their world in those."

"'Festival of the Dead,'" George repeated, shuddering. "Sounds kind of scary."

"It's not scary at all," Mick said, chuckling. "It's really just a big party."

One of the children was having problems getting her boat to float, so George knelt down to help.

"Let me assist, too, George," Gil offered, rolling up the sleeves of his *yukata*. "Sailing vessels have extremely tricky properties."

Mick turned to Nancy. "Do you want to check out the temple? It's one of the oldest in Tokyo."

"Sure," Nancy said eagerly.

As they walked, Mick said, "How's the case going? Have you and George made any progress since last night?"

"Yes and no," Nancy said, then brought him up to date on the missing diary, their adventures in Harajuku, and their meeting with Mad Dog Hayashi.

When she had finished, Mick looked puzzled. "What does it all mean?"

"It means that we've got another suspicious character to add to our list—Mad Dog," Nancy said grimly. "That makes two—three, if you include the guy who delivered the poisonous fugu. The problem is, I can't figure out how Mad Dog's involved in all this. And I don't have any solid proof to tie Midori's disappearance to either him or Yoko Nakamura."

"And what about the diary?" Mick added. "What would Mrs. Nakamura or Mad Dog or anyone else want with it?"

"Since I couldn't find any sign of forced entry, I'm starting to lean toward Mr. Kato's theory. Midori has a key, after all," Nancy pointed out. "Maybe Midori couldn't stand being without her diary. Or she wrote something in it that she didn't want anyone to see."

They had turned onto a narrow path lined with blooming magnolia trees. At the end of it was the temple, an ornate wooden structure. Mick and Nancy went to the entry, and found themselves all alone except for an old woman who was praying.

There was a silk sash hanging from one of the temple's rafters. The old woman pulled on it, and the sound of bells rang out in the air.

Nancy bent her head toward Mick's and whispered, "What's she doing?"

"Summoning the gods," Mick whispered back.

"Neat," Nancy said, then realized suddenly that her face was just inches away from Mick's.

Mick seemed to realize it, too. He fixed his eyes on hers for a brief, heart-stopping moment, then leaned over to kiss her.

"We've been looking all over for you two!"

Nancy and Mick jumped apart from each other guiltily. Gil was coming up to them, followed closely by George.

"There's a big bonfire out back," George announced.

Mick cleared his throat. "Actually, we—"

"We'd love to see the bonfire," Nancy cut in.

Mick stared at her, then broke into a grin. "Whatever you say, Nancy."

The bonfire turned out to be where all the action was. Nancy and her friends found hundreds of people dancing around it. A band consisting of drums, flutes, and several Japanese instruments Nancy couldn't identify provided the music.

"I think I'll sit this one out," Gil said apprehensively. "You all go ahead."

George sighed. "Come on, Gil. It's time you learned how to dance. Really, it's easy." She grabbed his arm and pulled him into the circle of dancers, ignoring Gil's protests.

They squeezed into one of the lines of dancers, and Nancy and Mick joined another. Nancy raised her arms and tried to imitate what everyone else was doing.

She discovered quickly that it was difficult to move, much less dance. People were crowded very close together, and somebody was bumping into her almost constantly. She felt like a sardine in a tin.

Then the music started growing louder and faster, and the dancers' movements more frenetic. Nancy felt almost hypnotized by the steady, throbbing beat. The flames of the bonfire cast an eerie glow over the scene.

"This is wild, isn't it?" Nancy cried out breathlessly to Mick. When there was no response, she stopped dancing and glanced around. "Mick?"

Nancy suddenly realized that she had somehow gotten pushed toward the center of the crowded circle, only a few feet from the bonfire. Mick, George, and Gil were nowhere to be seen.

She wiped a bead of sweat from her forehead, then called out, "Mick?"

Just then she felt a pair of strong hands grab her from behind. Before she could react, she was being shoved toward the bonfire—hard.

Nancy couldn't keep her balance. She fell toward the crackling flames.

"No!" she cried.

Chapter

Nine

Nancy felt a wave of heat wash over her as she stumbled toward the bonfire. The band was playing its frantic, macabre music faster and faster. The flames were inches away.

In the split second before landing in the fire, an image flashed in her mind. It was a move she'd learned in one of her martial arts classes. Without even thinking, she threw her left hand out. Her palm met dirt, and she pushed off it as hard as she could.

Nancy landed in a crumpled heap, a tiny flame singeing the edge of her *yukata* sleeve. She swatted at it, extinguishing it instantly. Then she struggled back to her feet, sweat pouring down her face, her heart thundering in her chest.

Someone just tried to kill me again, she

thought. She had to find her assailant before he—or she—got away.

Scanning the crowd, Nancy spotted a guy in a light blue *yukata* and straw hat. He was trying to squirm through the dancers, and he looked as though he were in a hurry.

That must be him, Nancy thought.

In all the confusion only a few dancers had even noticed Nancy's fall. Now, as she tried to push past them and pursue the guy in the blue *yukata,* they stared at her curiously and asked her if she was all right. None of them seemed to realize that she'd been pushed.

"I'm fine," Nancy said hastily. "Now, please, I have to get through."

The guy was fast approaching the outer edge of the circle when Nancy saw an arm reach out from somewhere, accidentally knocking his straw hat off. He had a crew cut, she noted.

The music had reached a fever pitch. Everyone was whirling and clapping wildly. "Oh, please," Nancy cried out in frustration as her path was blocked by two very energetic dancers.

By the time she made it out of the circle, Nancy's assailant was long gone.

At that moment Mick came rushing up to her. "I've been looking all over for you," he began, then stopped when he saw the expression on her face and the disheveled state of her clothes and hair. Without another word, he wrapped his arms around her and hugged her close.

Nancy shut her eyes and allowed herself to sink against his chest. Her knees felt wobbly, and her head was spinning.

"Let's get away from here," Mick suggested, taking her hand. He led her to a stone bench away from the noise of the band and the crowd. "What happened?" he asked gently.

Nancy told him, trying to keep her voice steady as she recounted the terrifying experience. "Did you get a look at the chap?" Mick asked worriedly.

"He was wearing a light blue *yukata* and a straw hat, and he had a crew cut," Nancy replied.

"Do any of your suspects have crew cuts?"

"Yes—Mad Dog Hayashi. And also the delivery guy who brought us the poisonous fugu." Nancy frowned. "Unless, of course, they're one and the same."

Mick's eyes flashed angrily. "Should we go to Hayashi's studio and confront him?"

"I'll pay him a visit first thing tomorrow," Nancy told him, brushing some dust off her *yukata*. "Right now all I want is a hot bath and a good night's sleep. Let's find Gil and George and get out of here."

It was Monday morning. George was sitting cross-legged on her futon, staring gloomily out at the back courtyard of the Sakura Ryokan. "Looks like our first rainy day, Nan," she remarked.

Nancy, who was standing at the closet, pulled a pink cotton sweater on over her baggy white T-shirt and joined her friend. The rain was beating steadily against the windowpane. Outside, the lush summer foliage quivered on the trees.

Nancy ran a hand through her reddish blond hair, which was curling ever so slightly from the humidity. "Actually, we've been really lucky so far," she murmured. "I think this is supposed to be the Japanese rainy season. This time of year it can pour for two weeks straight."

"Two weeks!" George exclaimed. "I hope that doesn't happen while we're here. We'll die of cabin fever."

Nancy chuckled. "No way. We're going to be too busy to stay inside. We have a case to solve, remember?"

"Right." George leaned back on her elbows and frowned. "After what happened to you at the festival, though, I'm beginning to wonder if we shouldn't pack our bags and go home." She added lightly, "Of course, that would mean leaving behind a certain gorgeous Australian."

Nancy felt her cheeks growing warm at the mention of Mick. He'd come so close to kissing her under the magnolia trees the night before.

What's wrong with you, Drew, she chided herself. You've got a fantastic boyfriend back home. And you told Mick that you just wanted to be friends.

There was a soft knock on the door. George went to get it. It was Mrs. Ito with the girls' breakfast.

"Good morning," she called out, setting the tray down on the table. "Have you found the young man who brought you the bad fugu yet?"

"Not yet," Nancy replied. "But we're working on it."

Mrs. Ito lifted the cover off one of the dishes. On it was a perfectly shaped golden omelet garnished with a sprig of parsley. "I thought you girls might be homesick for American food," she said.

George sat up eagerly. "Thank you, Mrs. Ito!"

After Mrs. Ito had left, George and Nancy sat down at the table and started to dig in. Smiling happily, George picked up a fork and took a bite of the omelet. Then her smile faded.

"Nan?" she said slowly. "This omelet is cold."

Nancy took a bite of hers and made a face. "You're right," she agreed. "I wonder if Mrs. Ito did that on purpose? Maybe she thinks omelets are supposed to be that way."

"Kind of makes me miss the grilled fish, rice, and miso soup we've been having every morning," George said.

The phone rang. Nancy went over to the dresser and picked it up. "Hello?"

"Nancy? It's me, Mari. Any news?"

"George and I had a pretty busy day yesterday," Nancy replied. Then she told Mari about

Harajuku, Mad Dog, and the Bon Matsuri festival.

Mari gasped when Nancy got to the part about the bonfire. "Nancy, this is getting crazy!"

"Someone does want me off this case," Nancy commented grimly. "The question is, who?"

"What are you going to do next?" Mari paused, then added, "Or maybe you should stop investigating, and we should just turn this whole mess over to the police. It's getting too dangerous—"

"Not yet," Nancy cut in. "I feel as if I'm getting close. George and I are going to pay Mad Dog another visit this morning. I have a strong hunch he may turn out to be the guy with the crew cut who's responsible for the fugu and the bonfire attack."

An hour later Nancy and George walked briskly across the vacant dirt lot toward Mad Dog's building, stepping carefully to avoid the puddles. The rain was coming down in sheets now, with occasional bursts of lightning and thunder.

They got to the front security door. But just as Nancy was about to open it, she heard footsteps inside. Somebody was coming down the stairs.

Could it be Mad Dog, Nancy wondered, then got an idea.

"Quick, George!" Nancy tugged at her friend's sleeve and dragged her toward the corner of the building. "We've got to hide!"

George obeyed instantly. A second later the security door was flung open and Mad Dog came stomping out. He was dressed in jeans and a black hooded sweatshirt. He glared at the rain, pulled his hood over his head, then started across the lot on foot.

"I want you to follow him," Nancy whispered to George. "I'm going to search his studio. So keep an eye on him, and make sure he doesn't come back right away. If he does, you'll have to distract him long enough for me to get out. Okay?"

"Okay, boss," George said, and set off across the lot.

Nancy set her umbrella down, then got her credit card out of her purse and started working on the lock. The door clicked open and she walked in.

Inside was a dimly lit concrete hallway. Off to the right was a red door, and to the left was a metal staircase. Nancy figured that Mad Dog's studio was on the second floor, since she'd heard him coming down the stairs.

She proceeded quietly to the second floor. At the top of the stairs was another hallway, and halfway down it, another red door. Nancy went up to it and tried the knob. Not surprisingly, it was locked—and with a complicated bolt lock to boot.

She reached into her purse for her lockpicking kit, glancing around nervously as she did. She noted that the hall was a dingy tan color with badly peeling paint. A few bare bulbs hung from the ceiling, bathing everything in a sickly yellow light. What a depressing place, she thought.

Nancy started to work on the lock. She hadn't gotten very far when she heard a strange noise coming from inside the studio. She froze and listened. There was a long silence—then, a few seconds later, the noise started again. It was a faint tapping sound, like that of fingers drumming against a tabletop.

Nancy moved closer to the door and pressed her ear against it, pushing her rain-drenched hair away from her face as she did. Then, before she knew what was happening, two powerful hands seized her shoulders, wrenched her away from the door, and flung her against the wall.

Pain shot through Nancy's back as it met the hard concrete. She sucked in a deep breath, trying to recover from the impact, then glanced up quickly. She found herself staring into Mad Dog's blazing eyes. His black hooded sweatshirt was soaking wet and clinging to his bulging chest and arms. George was nowhere in sight.

Mad Dog grabbed her shoulders again and pinned her tightly against the wall. "What do you think you're doing breaking into my studio?" he growled in a low, menacing voice.

"Let go of me," Nancy said in as calm a voice as possible.

His hands tightened on her shoulders. "Tell me what you're up to—now!"

Nancy's mind raced frantically, trying to find a way out of her predicament. And where was George? "I was coming to see you, to talk to you about Midori—" she began.

Mad Dog cut in angrily, "You were coming to see me with a lockpicking kit. Well, you're not the only one who carries useful tools." He pulled a Swiss army knife out of his jeans pocket and flicked open a small, sharp blade in one swift motion. He held the blade to Nancy's throat. "You tell me what you're up to right now, or I'll—"

"Stop it!" someone shouted.

Mad Dog's knife fell away from Nancy's throat. Nancy turned her head to see who had spoken. Mad Dog's door was open and a familiar figure was standing there.

It was Midori.

Chapter
Ten

Midori's gaze was fixed on Mad Dog. "Let go of her," she said sharply. "She's my friend."

Nancy was flooded with conflicting feelings—happiness, shock, relief. "Midori!" she burst out. "You're *okay!* But what are you doing here?"

Mad Dog loosened his grip on Nancy, but he didn't release her completely. "What if she's one of them?" he asked Midori doubtfully.

"She's *not* one of them," Midori replied tersely. "Now, please, Mad Dog—"

Mad Dog finally relented. "Are you all right?" he asked Nancy gruffly.

Nancy rubbed her shoulders. "I'll live," she murmured, then studied Midori with concern. The Japanese girl appeared to be unharmed, and yet she was even more haggard and pale than she had been on Friday. She looked as though she hadn't slept in ages.

"What's going on, Midori?" Nancy demanded. "Who is 'them'? We've all been so worried."

At that moment George came tearing up the stairs and down the hall. Her raincoat was dripping wet. "Nan, are you okay—" she began breathlessly, then stopped. She caught sight of Midori. "What on earth!" she gasped. Her eyes traveled from Midori to Mad Dog to Nancy. "What did I miss?" she asked.

"A lot," Nancy replied, managing a weak grin.

"I followed him, just like you said, but then I lost him in the rain," George admitted sheepishly. "I headed back here as soon as I realized it." She turned to Midori again. "Wow, Midori, am I ever glad to see you!"

Midori nodded. Her amber eyes were brimming with tears. "I've caused everyone so much trouble," she whispered hoarsely.

Nancy went up to her and put an arm around her. "Why don't we go inside and talk about it?" she suggested gently.

"Okay," Midori agreed, sniffling.

Once inside, the three girls sat down, and Mad Dog went to the kitchen to make tea.

Mad Dog's studio came as a surprise to Nancy. She'd expected it to be dark and moody, like its owner. Instead it was full of light and color and whimsy.

At one end of the enormous loft was a living room area. Instead of the usual furniture, there were hammocks hanging from the ceiling, vinyl lawn chairs, and TV trays that had been papier-mâchéd with American comic strips. In a pot near one of the many windows was a palm tree decorated with hundreds of small origami cranes.

At the far end was Mad Dog's painting area. Nancy could see that it was crammed with canvases, buckets, and brushes.

Midori followed Nancy's gaze. "Mad Dog is a terrific artist," she said. "He combines oil paint with all sorts of organic stuff—green tea, soy sauce, old vegetable peels." She pointed to a large painting on the wall behind them. It depicted a samurai warrior riding a motorcycle. "That's his."

"It's very Mad Dog," George remarked.

Nancy spotted the skinny black cat from the day before. It was crouched on a windowsill, watching everyone suspiciously.

"So that's Mad Dog's cat?" Nancy said to Midori. "We saw it outside when we came by yesterday."

"Mad Dog took him in this morning because of the rain," Midori explained. "He's a stray."

Nancy frowned. "Midori, if you decided you cared more for Mad Dog than for Ken, don't you think you—"

Midori sat up suddenly and interrupted. "No, Nancy. You've got it all wrong. Mad Dog and I are just friends."

"Friends?" George echoed.

"Yes," she went on, clearly desperate to convince them. "He took me in when . . ." Midori's voice trailed off.

"What, Midori?" Nancy said, leaning forward. "I know you're upset, but you've got to tell us about what."

Midori brushed at her eyes with the back of her hand. "It was an awful thing I did, running away from my wedding," she began shakily. "But I had no choice."

"What do you mean?" Nancy asked.

"It started last Thursday night," Midori said.

Nancy glanced at George, remembering Ken's account of that evening. "Go on," she told Midori.

"I went by Nakamura Incorporated at about five, to meet Ken." Nancy noticed the agony on Midori's face when she spoke his name.

"He came out to the reception area to tell me he was just finishing up an important meeting in his office," Midori continued. "He asked me to wait for him in the executive conference room."

Mad Dog reappeared with a steaming teapot and some cups. He set them down on one of the TV trays. "Are you certain you should be telling them this?" he asked Midori worriedly.

"It's okay, Mad Dog, really," Midori assured him, smiling slightly.

He cast doubtful glances at Nancy and George. "Whatever you say," he said. He poured the tea, handed everybody a cup, then sat down on the chair next to Midori's.

Nancy was struck by Mad Dog's protectiveness toward Midori.

"So then what happened?" George urged Midori.

"I went into the conference room," Midori said after taking a long sip of her tea. "It was empty, except for a big flat package sitting on the floor wrapped in brown paper. It looked like a painting, and I got all excited. I knew Ken's uncle Seiji collected art, and I thought it might be a famous work."

"So she wanted to peek at it," Mad Dog spoke up.

"I knelt down and started unwrapping part of it," Midori explained. "I figured a quick look wouldn't hurt anybody—I really just wanted to see what it was. But then Mr. Nakamura's assistant walked into the conference room, and he yelled at me to get away from it."

"Connor Drake," Nancy said, recalling Seiji Nakamura's cold, brusque assistant.

"I apologized to him, and then I asked him what the painting was," Midori said. "Either he didn't hear my question or he pretended not to.

He just picked up the package and rushed out of the room."

"That's weird," George commented.

Midori wrapped her hands around her teacup, as if trying to gather strength from its warmth. "I waited in the conference room for a few more minutes, alone. But Connor had upset me, and I wanted to talk to Ken. I decided to go to his office to see if his meeting was over."

She paused and took a deep breath. Mad Dog reached over and squeezed her shoulder encouragingly.

"The door was closed," Midori went on. "I pressed my ear up against it, to see what was going on before I knocked."

"Could you hear anything?" Nancy asked.

Midori stared at her for a long moment before replying, "Ken and Connor were in there. Ken was saying something like, 'Are you sure?' And Connor answered, 'Midori didn't see anything. But even if she did, so what? We can take care of the little troublemaker.' And then . . . Ken said . . ."

Midori covered her face with her hands and began to sob. "He said, 'We'll need to do more than scare her, though,'" she choked out.

"What!" Nancy gasped. She couldn't believe what she was hearing. "Midori, that's *awful!*"

Mad Dog handed Midori a paper napkin.

She took it from him and blew her nose. It was

a moment before she could go on. When she finally spoke, her voice was ragged.

"It was a nightmare," she whispered brokenly. "Two days before our wedding I find out that my fiancé is involved in something that is probably illegal—and that he's willing to do more than scare me because I happened to peek at a stupid painting!" She paused to blow her nose again. "I went straight home and locked myself in my room. Ken kept calling, but I had my mother tell him I wasn't feeling well."

"You must have been in total shock," George murmured sympathetically.

Midori nodded miserably. "I was. I thought about going to the police, but what could I tell them? I didn't have proof of anything. I didn't even know what Ken and Connor were up to. And I was so scared. I kept thinking, I couldn't do anything to make those guys suspicious, or I might get . . . they might . . ."

She dabbed at her eyes. "That's why I couldn't bring myself to tell my family or to cancel the wedding. I was afraid Ken and Connor would get wise to me."

"Did you think about just *talking* to Ken?" George asked.

"How could she?" Mad Dog cut in hotly. "I mean, how could she trust him? He betrayed her. For all she knew, something terrible would happen to her the second she said a word."

Nancy cradled her teacup in her hands. "So you decided that you had to go through with the wedding?" she asked Midori.

"I didn't see any way out," Midori replied. "I got as far as getting into my kimono. But then it occurred to me to just run away. It seemed to be the perfect solution—the *only* solution."

She glanced at Mad Dog and gave him a sad little smile. "I called Mad Dog. I knew he would help me. He came right away and whisked me back to his studio on his motorcycle."

"Good thing the traffic cops weren't out," Mad Dog mumbled. "I must have been going twice the speed limit both ways."

"You left the villa through the exit at the back of the property, right?" Nancy asked Midori. "We found a gold cord—your *obi-jime*—caught on the gate."

"We?" Midori became alarmed. "Who's 'we'?"

"Don't worry—it wasn't Ken or Connor," Nancy assured her. "You see, as soon as Mari figured out you were gone, she asked me to find you. She and George and I came across the *obi-jime.*"

"Oh." Midori sounded relieved. "Anyway, I've been staying here since Saturday, and Mad Dog's been taking care of me. That's why he was so rough with you in the hallway, Nancy. He was afraid you were one of Ken and Connor's spies."

Mad Dog looked at Midori a little guiltily. "I

didn't tell you that your friends showed up here yesterday. I didn't want to worry you."

Nancy asked him straight out. "You didn't deliver a batch of poisonous fugu to our *ryokan* room? Or push me into the bonfire at a Bon Matsuri festival?"

Mad Dog's eyes widened. "Never."

"Somebody did these things to you, Nancy?" Midori asked anxiously.

"Yes," Nancy replied, and told her and Mad Dog about everything that had happened since Saturday.

When she got to the part about the stolen diary, Mad Dog held up a hand. "I'm guilty of that. Midori asked me to sneak into her house late Saturday night and get the thing."

"I'd written some stuff about Ken and Connor in it," Midori explained hastily. "I didn't want them to get hold of it."

"That explains why there were no signs of a break-in," Nancy said, nodding. "You gave Mad Dog your key." She paused, then added, "The guy who delivered the fugu and pushed me into the bonfire was Japanese and had a crew cut. Since Ken doesn't have a crew cut, he and Connor must have somebody else working for them."

Midori acted confused. "But why would they try to hurt you, Nancy?"

"They must not want me to find you," Nancy

said, her blue eyes flashing. "They probably think that your running away was connected to last Thursday night somehow. So either they're looking for you themselves, or they're hoping you'll stay in hiding and keep your mouth shut."

Midori shuddered. "I understand."

"The key is that painting," Nancy went on. "It must be a really valuable work, or Ken and Connor wouldn't be making such a big deal out of it. Did you recognize it, Midori?"

"I saw only a small part of the right side," Midori replied. "All I can tell you is that it was a medium-size oil, about two feet by three feet. It looked like an Impressionist or Postimpressionist landscape to me—lots of sky blue on top, bright colors on the bottom, fluttery brushstrokes. Oh, and I saw the end of a signature—the letter *T* in red."

"That's a start," Nancy said. "Listen, Midori. You'd better stay here for a while. We don't want Ken and Connor to find you. George and I will try to track down the painting."

Mad Dog leaned forward and grinned at her. It was the first time Nancy had seen him happy. "Hey, that would be great," he said gratefully. "I wasn't sure how I was going to watch over Midori and find a way to nail those guys at the same time."

Midori clasped Nancy's hand. "You're such a good friend, Nancy," she murmured. "But I don't want to put you in any more danger."

"I can take care of myself," Nancy told her. "But what should we do about Mari? Should I tell her where you are?"

Midori thought for a moment, then said, "Yes, and tell her that I'm okay. I don't want her to worry about me." She paused. "But tell her to keep the information to herself, and that she shouldn't call me or come here, no matter what. I don't want to involve her in any of this or risk having anyone follow her here."

"So you don't want us to explain to her about the painting, or about Ken and Connor?" Nancy said.

"That's right," Midori replied firmly. "The less she knows, the better."

"In this situation, ignorance is definitely bliss," George agreed.

"You've got a gleam in your eye, Nancy Drew," Mick said. "What's up? I know you didn't ask me out to lunch just to hear me talk about the wonderful world of investment banking. You've got something on your mind, don't you?"

Nancy and Mick were sitting at a corner table in a sushi restaurant. George had gone back to the *ryokan* to get in a quick jog. The morning's storm had stopped, and through the open window Nancy could see a beautiful rainbow.

"You're very clever, Mick Devlin," Nancy replied, chuckling. "If you ever get sick of your job, you should consider a career in detective work. I'd be happy to give you a reference."

A waiter appeared at their table just then. "Are you ready to order?" he asked them in Japanese.

Nancy scanned the menu quickly. "I'd like the lunch special with the tuna rolls," she said.

"That sounds great," Mick said. "I'd like the exact same thing."

The waiter went away and came back immediately with two small salads.

Mick separated his wooden chopsticks and started in on his salad. "So tell me what's going on," he said between bites. "I love this ginger dressing."

Nancy ate some of her salad. "Me, too."

Mick's green eyes sparkled. "That clinches it, Nancy. We like the same sushi, the same kind of dressing—" He raised his eyebrows playfully. "What do you say? Why don't you come to your senses and be my girlfriend?"

Nancy reached across the table and put her hand on his arm. "That's exactly what I had in mind," she said very seriously.

Chapter

Eleven

MICK PUT HIS CHOPSTICKS DOWN and gaped at Nancy. "You want to be my girlfriend," he said finally. Then he shook his head and gave her a radiant smile. "That's the best news I've heard in a long time. I have to admit I'm a little surprised, though. You told me at Puppy Love Live that you and Ned were—"

"Yes, I know," Nancy cut in quickly. She hesitated before going on. She knew her plan was dangerous, and Mick was looking at her so tenderly that she almost wished she *could* be his girlfriend.

Stick to business, Drew, she told herself sternly. "I still mean what I said," she went on after a moment. "But there's been a major break in the case, and I need a way to check out Nakamura

99

Incorporated. I figure the best way to do that would be to pose as your girlfriend. I could meet you there for a date."

Disappointment was reflected in Mick's eyes, but only for a second. He leaned forward and winked at her. "You picked the right chap for the job, Nancy. I'll see to it that we make a very convincing couple."

Nancy felt a blush creep over her cheeks. "Thanks, Mick."

"So you want to snoop around Nakamura Incorporated, eh?" Mick said. "But why?"

"This is absolutely top secret—for your ears only, okay?" Nancy said in a low voice. Then she told him about finding Midori at Mad Dog's studio and repeated everything Midori had told her about Ken and Connor.

When she had finished, Mick appeared even more astonished than before. "Ken Nakamura and Connor Drake are pulling off some scam involving a painting? That's incredible."

"Why incredible?" Nancy asked.

Mick shrugged. "Ken always struck me as such a straight arrow. He's already loaded. Plus I had the impression that he and Connor didn't get along too well." He hesitated. "Actually, that's not right. It's Ken and his *uncle* who don't seem to get along, and I just figured that Connor, being Mr. Nakamura's assistant, wouldn't be one of Ken's favorite people, either."

"Ken doesn't get along with his uncle?" Nancy repeated, puzzled.

"At a couple of meetings they've had disagreements about deals," Mick said. "They don't seem to see eye to eye on things."

The waiter came by with their sushi. It was arranged on boat-shaped bamboo platters and garnished with paper-thin lemon slices.

"So what do you think this painting business can be about?" Mick asked Nancy as they started in on the sushi.

"Your guess is as good as mine," Nancy said. "What are the usual art-related crimes? Smuggling, theft, forgery—"

"Maybe the painting is a fake," Mick suggested. "That would explain why Connor freaked out when he saw Midori studying it. He might have figured an ex-art student would be able to tell an imitation from the real thing."

"That's a possibility," Nancy said thoughtfully. "So you won't mind helping me out, Mick? I know it's kind of odd, having to pose as my boyfriend and all."

Mick reached across the table and squeezed her hand. "Why would I mind? Posing as your boyfriend will be great." He brought her hand to his lips and kissed each finger lightly. "See? I'm having fun already," he added, grinning mischievously.

Nancy reluctantly pulled her hand away and

tried to ignore the racing of her heart. Was this crazy plan going to work? she wondered. How could she just pretend to be Mick's girlfriend when a small part of her wanted it for real? And what about Ned, who was there for her back in the States?

"So, when can I come by your office?" Nancy asked, trying to keep her voice level. "The sooner, the better."

"Tonight?" Mick said. "Why don't you come around five, say, to meet me for dinner? A lot of the employees leave at four thirty, so things should be pretty quiet by then."

"That sounds perfect," Nancy replied.

Mick gave her a lazy smile. "It's a date."

The Nakamura Incorporated offices occupied several floors of a building in the posh neighborhood of Akasaka. The reception area on the sixth floor, where Mick had told Nancy to ask for him, was decorated in modern Japanese style, with teak walls, gray slate floors, and sleek black leather couches. There was a miniature goldfish pond in one corner, complete with a tiny waterfall.

It was exactly five o'clock. As Nancy waited for Mick, she listened to the soothing sound of the trickling water and felt her eyelids start to close. Her jet lag was catching up with her.

"Nancy!"

Her eyelids flew open. Mick was standing in front of her, his arms outstretched. "Oh, hi, Mick," she murmured.

Mick lifted Nancy by the hands, and before she could stop him he was hugging her tightly. "You look beat, darling," he said sympathetically. "Do you want to cancel our date?"

Nancy started to pull away from him, but then realized that the receptionist was watching them. Oh, boy, she thought, putting her arms around Mick's neck and hugging him back. What am I getting myself into?

When they finally separated, Nancy smiled weakly at him. "Of course I don't want to cancel our date, *darling*. I've been looking forward to it all day."

"Great." Mick took her hand and led her through a set of double doors. "I'll give you the VIP tour first," he said in a low voice. "The layout is pretty typical—a circular hallway, offices all around the perimeter of the circle, and two conference rooms inside the circle."

He pointed out a long line of video monitors in the hallway. They were flashing codes and numbers. "Stock activity in all the major markets of the world," he explained.

"There aren't too many people here—just as you said," Nancy noted as they walked.

"I think just about everybody's gone except for the head honchos," Mick replied. "Connor, Mr.

Nakamura, and Ken are in the executive conference room with some clients."

Nancy's eyes lit up. This would be the perfect opportunity to search Ken and Connor's offices.

Mick glanced around, made sure no one was nearby, then whispered, "So what have you and George been up to since I saw you at lunch?"

"We've been trying to track down a painting," Nancy whispered back. "George and I went to the library and came up with a list of Impressionists and Postimpressionists whose last names end in the letter *T.*"

"And who did you come up with?" Mick prodded.

"Claude Monet, Georges Seurat, Edouard Manet, Mary Cassatt, Berthe Morisot—just to name a few," Nancy replied. "George is over at Mad Dog's right now. She's running them by Midori, to see if any of them rings a bell."

"Have you told Mari about her sister yet?" Mick asked.

Nancy nodded. "I talked to her this afternoon. She was really glad to hear that Midori's okay, but she wasn't happy about all the secrecy. I made her swear not to tell anybody anything, though, or to try to contact Midori."

"So she doesn't know about Ken and Connor?" Mick said.

"No," Nancy said. "Midori wanted it that way. If you run into Mari, don't say a word."

"Understood." Mick peered at his watch. "Listen, Nancy—can I leave you alone for about fifteen minutes? I promised one of our clients to give her a call."

"No problem," Nancy said. "You said Ken and Connor were in a meeting, right? Just show me their offices, and I'll take it from there."

Mick explained how to find them. "And mine is this one here," he finished, pointing. "I'll see you in a little while. Be careful, okay?"

"I'll be fine," Nancy reassured him.

Fortunately, there was no one around the two offices. Nancy decided to search Ken's first. She noticed a framed photograph of Midori on his desk. It struck her as surprising that he'd kept it after what had happened.

Working efficiently, Nancy went through some papers and files. She then began going through his Rolodex, hoping to find the name of a gallery that might be linked to the painting. All the entries were in Japanese and were hard for Nancy to decipher.

Then she got a hunch and headed for Connor's office.

Just as Nancy had guessed, Connor's Rolodex was in English. "Bingo," she said softly, and began flipping through the cards.

Halfway through the Rolodex, she found entries for two auction houses: Minamoto Auctions and Nobu Auctioneers Limited. Thinking they might handle art, she quickly jotted down their addresses and phone numbers and stuffed the piece of paper into her pocket.

She had returned to the Rolodex and started on the *O* entries when she was interrupted by a deep male voice.

"What are you doing in here?" he asked in Japanese.

Nancy's hand froze on the Rolodex. She turned slowly. Ken was standing in the doorway.

Chapter
Twelve

NANCY GAVE KEN an apologetic smile. "Hi," she said sweetly. "I know this looks odd. But this is the first opportunity I've had to go through Mick's Rolodex without him hanging around."

Ken stopped in his tracks. "Mick's Rolodex!" he burst out. "That isn't Mick's Rolodex—it's Connor's!"

Nancy gasped. "You mean I'm not in Mick's office? Oh, no, I feel so stupid. I guess the circular hallway got me all mixed up."

"Mick's in the interns' office four doors down," Ken said, then stared at her suspiciously. "Why would you want to go through his Rolodex?"

Nancy giggled nervously. "It's kind of embarrassing, but—oh, well, I guess I can tell you. You see, Mick and I have been seeing each other for a while—long distance, of course. We met in Geneva, you know."

"No, I didn't know," Ken replied coolly.

"But for a while now I've suspected that he had another girlfriend," Nancy went on, adding a hurt edge to her voice. "I wanted to find out for sure. I thought that her name and phone number might be in his Rolodex."

Ken was silent for a moment. "So this has nothing to do with your search for Midori?" he asked finally.

"Of course not!" Nancy protested. "Why would anyone here know anything about Midori's disappearance?" She watched Ken's reaction before going on. His expression never changed.

"By the way, what are you doing in Connor's office?" Nancy asked casually, trying to shift the focus away from herself. "Are you looking for something, too?"

Ken blushed. "Of course not. He asked me to meet him here." He peered at his watch. "My uncle must be keeping him for some reason."

"Well, I'd better run," Nancy said, heading for the door. "Mick will be wondering about me." She paused at Ken's side. "Listen, could we keep this little incident between us? I don't want Mick to know what I've been up to."

Not waiting for Ken's reply, she breezed out the door—only to run smack into Connor.

The stocky, red-haired Englishman stepped back and glared at her. "What are you—"

"Oh, hello," Nancy mumbled hastily. "Nice to see you again." Then she continued down the hall.

As she rounded the curve in the hall, she glanced over her shoulder. The two men were standing in the doorway of Connor's office, staring at her and talking. She couldn't hear what they were saying, but they looked very serious.

"Darling, where have you been? I've been looking everywhere for you!"

Nancy stopped and whirled around. Mick was walking toward her.

Nancy rushed up to him. "Hi!" she said loudly. "I'm starving—can we go now?"

They started down the hall toward the reception area. When they'd gotten completely out of Connor and Ken's earshot, Mick said, "So what happened?"

"Plenty," Nancy said, and filled him in.

Mick laughed when she got to the part about his "other girlfriend." "That was a good one, Nancy. I'm sure you made it sound convincing, too."

"I hope so," Nancy said a little doubtfully. "Listen—do you know anything about either of these auction houses?" She showed him the piece of paper she had put in her pocket.

"Minamoto and Nobu," Mick read. "No, not

really. But according to these addresses, they're both pretty close by."

"I'll try them first thing in the morning. I want to see if the painting Midori saw might have come from either place." Nancy stuffed the piece of paper back in her pocket. "Now, I meant what I said before—I really am starving. Should we get a quick bite to eat? My treat."

Mick shook his head. "As your boyfriend, I not only get to kiss you as often as I want, but I pick up the checks," he teased.

When they got to the reception area, they found Yoko Nakamura. She was sitting on one of the black leather couches leafing through a magazine.

She looked up at Nancy and Mick and gave them a cold little smile. "Ms. Drew. Mr. Devlin."

Nancy forced herself to smile back. "It's nice to see you, Mrs. Nakamura," she said politely. "Are you waiting for someone?"

"I'm waiting for Seiji, if you must know," Yoko replied. "We're attending some tedious banquet for one of his politician friends."

At that moment the double doors swung open and Seiji strolled into the reception area. Nancy noted again the similarities between him and Ken—the square, tanned face and tall, slender build.

He greeted Mick and Nancy. "I didn't realize you two knew each other," he said.

Mick wrapped his arm around Nancy. "We go back a long way," he said simply.

Yoko set her magazine aside and stood up. "Let's go, Seiji," she said impatiently. "We're going to be late."

The four of them crowded into an elevator.

"So how are you enjoying Tokyo, Ms. Drew?" Seiji asked. He took off his rimless glasses, rubbed them briskly against his elegant charcoal gray suit, and put them back on. "It's a wonderful city, isn't it?"

Nancy stared at him. He seemed a little nervous, she thought. Was his nephew's ill-fated wedding still on his mind?

"Tokyo is great," she replied after a second. "There's so much to do here."

They continued making small talk until they'd gotten out of the building. Then Seiji and Yoko bid Nancy and Mick goodbye and disappeared into a waiting limousine.

Nancy turned to Mick. "Where to now?"

"Well, I know this little karaoke place—" Mick said.

Then something caught Nancy's eye. Through the glass doors of the Nakamura Incorporated building, she could see Connor emerging from one of the elevators. In a few seconds he would come outside and see Nancy and Mick on the sidewalk.

"Mick," she whispered urgently. "Connor

Drake is coming. Quick, let's act like we're a couple."

"Let's," Mick agreed, and before Nancy knew what was happening he grabbed her and kissed her on the lips.

Nancy's first instinct was to pull back. Then another instinct took over, and she felt herself melting into the kiss. It seemed to go on forever, and it was wonderful. It brought back memories of Greece, of the night Mick had proposed to her on a secluded, moonlit hill.

When she finally stepped back, her cheeks were flushed and her heart was pounding wildly. "Mick," she said breathlessly. "We can't—"

Connor passed by them at that moment. He pretended not to notice them as he stepped to the curb and waved down a cab.

"Have sushi again. Let's go someplace else instead," Nancy finished, watching Connor carefully.

Mick grinned and took her hand. "Anything you say."

Later that night Nancy and George were enjoying a bath in the Sakura Ryokan's huge sunken tub.

"This sure beats my usual thirty-second shower at the gym," George remarked, cupping some water in her hands and pouring it over her head.

Nancy leaned back against the edge of the tub

and closed her eyes. "The water is really hot, but once you get used to it, it's great."

"I wish my bathroom at home looked like this," George added.

Nancy opened her eyes. The bathroom was gorgeous—ice blue tiles, bamboo buckets full of perfumed soaps and shampoos, pots of purple and white orchids that seemed to thrive in the steamy environment. A cool breeze wafted in through the open window, providing a welcome contrast to the heat of the bath.

"So tell me about Midori," Nancy said after a while. "Did she narrow down our list of artists?"

"Sorry," George said, frowning. "Midori said it could have been any of them. She just didn't see enough of the painting." She added, "How about you? How did things go at Nakamura Incorporated?"

Nancy filled her in on her adventures in Connor's office. "I want to visit the two auction houses tomorrow morning," she finished. "They may be totally unrelated to the case, but they're definitely worth checking out."

"Absolutely," George said. "Hey, how did your cover as Mick's girlfriend work out?"

Nancy felt her cheeks turning pink. "It was okay," she replied hastily, then tried to change the subject. "Oh, did I tell you where he took me after we were through at Nakamura? A karaoke restaurant."

"Neat," George said.

Nancy rose out of the water slightly and reached for a loofah sponge. "It was fun. We—"

Nancy heard a high-pitched whizzing sound. Instinctively she ducked as a shiny star-shaped object flew toward her head.

Chapter

Thirteen

THE SHINY OBJECT missed Nancy by inches and neatly decapitated one of the orchid plants behind her.

"What was *that?*" George whispered hoarsely.

Without wasting a second, Nancy got out of the bath, put on her *yukata,* and rushed over to the open window. She managed to catch a glimpse of someone fleeing from the dark courtyard. It was a man with a crew cut—the same one from the Bon Matsuri festival!

A moment later Nancy heard the sound of a motorcycle revving up, then speeding away.

"It was our friend with the crew cut," Nancy said gravely, turning from the window. "And unless I'm wrong, he tried to finish me off with a *shuriken.*"

"A what?" George repeated.

Nancy walked over to the orchid plant and picked up the shiny star-shaped piece of metal lying next to it. "It's a weapon used by ninjas— Japanese assassins," she explained. "Each point of the star is a lethal blade."

George turned white. "Nancy, you could have been . . . you were almost . . ."

"I know," Nancy said quietly. "Listen, let's get out to the courtyard to see if the guy left any clues."

A thorough search turned up nothing. "He's just like a ninja," Nancy remarked. "He moves quickly and quietly, and leaves no traces."

George shivered in her thin *yukata*. "What are we going to do, Nan?" she said anxiously. "This case is getting more dangerous by the minute. Maybe we should just go to the police."

Nancy shook her head. "I want to get some evidence against Ken and Connor before we do that. Besides, I think we're close to a breakthrough. Let's just hang on a little while longer, okay?"

George sighed. "Okay."

"This *shuriken* attack means that Ken didn't buy my story about looking for Mick's other girlfriend," Nancy said as she and George headed back into the *ryokan*. "In fact, catching me at Connor's Rolodex must have made him realize that I've found Midori and that she told me about the painting. Otherwise, why would I be snooping around Connor's office, right?"

"Right," George agreed.

"It also told him that Midori knows more about their little scam than he and Connor originally thought," Nancy went on. "And that she ran away from their wedding because of it. He must have wondered about that."

"He and Connor are probably desperate to find Midori now," George noted. "I hate to think of what would happen if they discovered the Mad Dog connection."

"They're not *going* to discover it," Nancy said firmly. "Not if we can help it."

The next morning Nancy and George walked out of Minamoto Auctions and into the sunlight.

"One down, one to go," George said. "I hope we have better luck at the other place."

"At least that was a fast stop," Nancy pointed out. "The fact that Minamoto only handles antique furniture knocks them right off our list. They can't be connected to our painting."

"It's a little scary being so close to Nakamura Incorporated, isn't it?" George murmured, watching several people pass her on the crowded sidewalk. "I hope we don't run into anybody."

"Me, too." Nancy replied.

The other auction house, Nobu Auctioneers Limited, was right around the corner. It was housed in a sleek one-story building made of blue-green reflective glass. A large abstract sculpture stood next to the entrance.

"The sculpture's a good sign," Nancy said to George in a low voice. "It looks like Nobu *is* in the art auction business."

Nancy's guess proved to be correct. Inside the lobby were dozens of posters advertising auctions of European and Asian art.

Scanning the posters, Nancy wondered if Ken and Connor might have bought their painting at one of the Nobu auctions. But if that were the case, why all the secrecy and intrigue? And why were they so afraid of what Midori might know?

Nancy approached the young woman sitting at the semicircular chrome reception desk. "Excuse me. Would it be possible to see the catalogs of your most recent shows? Say, going back a month?"

"Certainly," the young woman said, studying Nancy from behind her lavender-tinted glasses. "You can return them to me when you are finished." She handed Nancy four glossy booklets.

Nancy and George sat down on a bench on the far side of the lobby.

"Pretty fancy," George murmured, glancing around.

Nancy held up one of the catalogs. "Hey, this looks good. It's for an auction of Impressionist and Postimpressionist paintings that took place last Wednesday, the day before Midori saw the painting at Nakamura Incorporated!"

Nancy and George started going through the catalog eagerly. There were nearly a hundred entries. Each entry consisted of a small color reproduction of the work for sale along with a short description of it.

"Remember—we need an oil painting by an artist whose name ends in the letter *T*," Nancy reminded George. "It's probably a landscape, about two feet by three feet, with sky blue on top and lots of color on the bottom. And the signature will be in the lower right-hand corner, in red."

"Hey, there's a Monet," George said, pointing at one of the entries. Then she looked close and shook her head. "No, skip it. It's not anything like the painting Midori described."

By the time they'd gotten through the catalog, they'd come across only two landscapes fitting Midori's specifications—a van Gogh and a Pissarro. But they hadn't found any by artists whose names ended with the letter *T*.

"What a disappointment, huh, Drew?" George grumbled, snapping the catalog shut. "I thought we were on to something here."

"Me, too," Nancy said. "Let's try the other catalogs." Then she sat up suddenly. "Wait a minute."

George frowned. "What?"

"I just remembered—Vincent van Gogh always signed his paintings with his *first* name, not his last," Nancy explained. "Here, give me that catalog. Let's take another look at his landscape."

Nancy turned to the page quickly, held it up to the light, and squinted. She could make out a tiny signature on the lower right—in red!

"This must be it," Nancy said to George excitedly.

She got up and rushed over to the receptionist. "Excuse me," she said. "Can you tell me who bought this van Gogh at last Wednesday's auction?"

The receptionist smiled politely at her. "I'm sorry, that is confidential."

"I see," Nancy said, trying to mask her disappointment. "Well, then—would it be possible for me to keep this catalog? You see, I love this van Gogh painting."

"I'm sorry," the receptionist said, still smiling. "We only have a few copies left of that catalog, and I'm not authorized to give them out."

As soon as Nancy and George were out of the building, George said, "Now what? There's no way to prove Ken and Connor bought that painting—"

"Yes, there is," Nancy said with a determined glint in her eye. "Come on—we've got to find a phone booth."

Nancy's first call was to Midori.

After exchanging greetings, Nancy went on to

describe the van Gogh landscape in the Nobu catalog. "Does that sound like the painting you saw?"

"Yes!" Midori replied instantly. "Now that you mention it, it looked a lot like a van Gogh. I should have thought of that myself."

"Great," Nancy said eagerly. "Now, I just have to get some solid evidence tying that painting to Ken and Connor, and we're halfway there."

After promising to keep Midori posted, Nancy made a call to Mick.

"How nice to hear your voice," he said softly. "What can I do for you? A stock transfer? A candlelit dinner for two?"

"The dinner sounds nice," she replied, meaning it. "But first I have a little assignment for you. I have to warn you, though—it's a little tricky."

"The trickier, the better," Mick replied.

"And it might be dangerous," Nancy added. "Things have been really heating up since I saw you last night." She told him about the *shuriken* incident.

Mick was dismayed. "Are you okay, Nancy? If anything happened to you—"

"I'm fine," Nancy told him gently. "Not a scratch on me."

"I'm glad to hear it," Mick said huskily. He cleared his throat. "Okay—so what's my assignment?"

"Well, first, you're going to have to practice

speaking Japanese with a British accent," Nancy began.

An hour later, at noon, Nancy, George, and Mick met at a bus shelter across the street from Nobu Auctioneers. George had been standing at that spot since eleven. Nancy had gone back to the *ryokan* and changed into a tailored silk suit.

"How did it go?" Nancy asked Mick.

"I followed your instructions to the letter," Mick said with a grin. "I phoned the accountant at Nobu and told him I was Connor Drake, calling on behalf of Mr. Nakamura. I told the chap—his name was Mr. Soseki, incidentally— that my absentminded new secretary accidentally lost the paperwork from last Wednesday's purchase and that I was most anxious to have it replaced right away."

"And you asked him if it would be okay to have your secretary come by and pick it up?" Nancy said.

"Of course," Mick replied. "He said that he would leave the duplicate documents with the receptionist."

"Nice going, Mick," Nancy said excitedly. "Now we know for sure that Ken and Connor bought that van Gogh." She turned to George. "What about the receptionist with the purple glasses? Has she left for lunch yet?"

"I saw her leave the building fifteen minutes ago with two other women," George said. "I think this is your chance, Nan. You'd better get in there and get the papers before she gets back and blows your act sky-high."

Nancy nodded and started across the street. "Wish me luck, guys."

"Be careful," George called out.

Nancy stepped into the Nobu building and approached the semicircular reception desk. A young man was sitting there, leafing through an art magazine.

He raised his eyes to Nancy. "May I help you?"

"I'm Connor Drake's secretary, from Nakamura Incorporated," Nancy replied smoothly. "I'm here to pick up some papers for him from Mr. Soseki."

The young guy nodded. "Just one second, please." He picked up the phone, punched in a four-digit number, and spoke a few rapid Japanese phrases into it.

Nancy felt a twinge of fear. "Is there a problem?" she asked him after he'd hung up. "I was told that the papers would be waiting for me right here."

"Just one second, please," the young guy repeated.

Nancy glanced around. There was a group of elegantly dressed women standing at the elevator bank. Then the elevator doors opened, and two men came out. One of them was a gray-haired man in a brown suit. The other was a security guard.

The gray-haired man had an angry expression on his face. Oh, no, Nancy thought. Mr. Soseki must have spoken to the real Connor Drake and found out that the request for duplicate paperwork was totally bogus.

The gray-haired man was approaching her fast, the security guard at his heels. "You there!" he called out.

Chapter
Fourteen

THE GRAY-HAIRED MAN stopped beside her. "You're from Mr. Drake's office?"

Nancy stared at him and forced herself to smile. "Well—" she began.

Not waiting for her reply, the man reached into his jacket and pulled out a manila envelope. "This was supposed to be waiting up here for you," he said tightly. "But my assistant went off to lunch without taking care of it. I'm terribly sorry. I'll be sure to speak to her when she returns." He added, "By the way, I am Mr. Soseki."

"Oh," Nancy said, relieved. "I'm, um, Ms. Marvin."

The security guard strode right past Nancy and Mr. Soseki and leaned over the reception desk.

"You can tell the second-shift guy when he comes in that I couldn't wait around for him any longer," Nancy heard him say to the receptionist in Japanese.

So the guard hadn't been interested in her at all! Nancy thought. She felt an irresistible urge to chuckle, but she stifled it and said, "Well, thank you, Mr. Soseki. You can be sure that Mr. Drake won't forget this."

"My pleasure," Mr. Soseki replied, bowing.

Nancy tucked the manila envelope into her purse and headed for the door. She spotted the other receptionist, the one with the lavender-tinted glasses, walking toward the building with two other women.

In one quick motion Nancy reached into her purse, found her sunglasses, and slipped them on. Then she started across the street as casually as possible. The receptionist didn't seem to notice her.

George and Mick were the only ones at the bus shelter. "Success?" George asked Nancy.

"So far, so good," Nancy replied. She got the manila envelope out of her purse and pulled out its contents—a complicated-looking two-page form, all in Japanese.

Nancy turned to Mick. "Can you translate this?" she asked him. "It would take me too long."

Mick studied the form quickly. "It's the bill of sale for the van Gogh landscape," he explained.

"The buyer is listed as Nakamura Incorporated. The seller isn't named. The price is"—he paused and whistled—"the equivalent of fifteen million U.S. dollars."

"Wow," George said.

"The buyer is Nakamura Incorporated?" Nancy repeated. "Not Ken or Connor?"

"Right," Mick said.

"That's strange," Nancy remarked. "Mick, is it possible for Ken or Connor to use Nakamura funds without getting authorization?"

"I wouldn't really know about that," Mick replied, shrugging. He read over the bill of sale again. "You know, there's something about this painting that rings a bell. I think I read an article about it in the paper, maybe two or three weeks ago." He sighed. "I wish I could remember what it was."

"That sounds promising," Nancy said eagerly. "I'd like to go to the library and track the article down."

Mick glanced at his watch. "I wish I could help you, but I'd better get back to work. I've got reports to do."

"Poor Mick," Nancy murmured. "Listen, you've already helped us plenty. I'll call you soon with a progress report."

After saying goodbye, Nancy and George headed for the library. They got a pile of English-language newspapers from the librarian and settled down at a long wooden table.

"If we strike out with these, we can try the Japanese-language papers later, with Mick's help," Nancy said to George.

"Good idea," George said, picking up one of the papers. "We're just looking for any mention of the van Gogh, right?"

"Right," Nancy replied.

"Here's something," George said after a while. She pointed out a small article to Nancy. "Some politician named Watanabe bought the very same painting just two weeks ago."

Nancy scanned the article. "It says that Watanabe bought it at a private sale conducted by Nobu Auctioneers Limited for—" She paused, mentally converting the yen amount into dollars. "The equivalent of ten million! But that doesn't make sense. How could the painting have gone up in value by five million dollars in just two weeks?"

"And it's weird that Watanabe wanted to get rid of it so quickly," George piped up. "I mean, two weeks is barely enough time to figure out where to hang it."

"It's strange, too, that this Watanabe wasn't named on the bill of sale I got from Mr. Soseki," Nancy added. She read the newspaper article one more time. "What do Ken and Connor have to do with all of this, anyway? And what do they think Midori knows that's got them so afraid?"

"Too many unanswered questions," George grumbled.

Nancy stood up. "You're right about that, George. Let's head back to the *ryokan* and go over every piece of this case again. We're going to figure out what Ken and Connor are up to if it takes us all day and night."

Nancy and George were sitting cross-legged on the floor of their room when the phone rang.

Nancy went over to the dresser and picked it up. "Hello?"

"Nancy?" It was Mick. "I have to see you and George right away."

The urgency in his voice startled Nancy. "Where are you?" she asked him. She glanced at her watch and noted that it was after six o'clock.

"I'm at the office," Mick replied tersely. "But I don't want you to come here. There's a little diner around the corner from me called Happiness Cup."

"We're on our way," Nancy said. Then she added, "Are you all right?"

"I'm fine," Mick said. "Just get there as soon as you can, okay?"

Half an hour later Nancy and George were sitting across from Mick in a red vinyl booth. After the waitress had brought them some water and taken their orders, Mick leaned across the table and said, "Connor Drake is dead."

Nancy gasped. "What!"

"Just before I phoned you, Gil came into the interns' office and told me. Now everybody at

Nakamura is talking about it," Mick went on. "Apparently Connor was going too fast on some road outside the city. He lost control of the wheel and went over an embankment."

"How horrible!" George cried out.

Mick glanced around quickly, then said in a low voice, "How *unbelievable* is more like it. Connor was a car buff. He collected vintage cars."

"What does that have to do with it?" George asked him, puzzled.

"The accident happened in his favorite car, this big old American convertible," Mick explained. "The thing is, he was so careful about not getting one scratch on it that he never drove it over thirty miles an hour. I know this because he took me and Gil for a ride in it once."

Nancy's eyes widened. "Are you suggesting that Connor's death wasn't an accident?"

Mick nodded. "Besides, what was Connor doing on a road outside Tokyo in the middle of a workday?"

Nancy tried to digest this startling information. She rested her chin on her hands. "Who could have wanted Connor dead? And how does his death fit into the case?"

Mick took a sip of water. "Any ideas?"

"Well, we do have a new angle," Nancy replied, and told him about the article she and George had found in the library. "So now we know that Ken and Connor are connected to this politician,

Watanabe, through the van Gogh. But we still don't know what the connection is."

The waitress appeared at their table with three bowls of noodles. "Enjoy," she said.

The three of them fell into a thoughtful silence as they started eating their food.

Some shadowy memory was hovering at the edge of Nancy's mind—something having to do with the case. She frowned, trying to remember.

"Gil," she said suddenly.

Mick and George looked up from their noodles. "What?" they said in unison.

Nancy leaned forward eagerly. "George, before the Bon Matsuri festival, you told me Gil liked talking about things like—"

"Superconductors," George finished for her, rolling her eyes. "And the role of the Japanese art market in illegal political contributions." She smiled wryly at Mick. "Your friend's a real smart guy."

"But what was Gil telling you about these political contributions, George?" Nancy persisted. "What was the connection to the art market?"

"To tell you the truth, I wasn't really listening," George admitted.

Mick slapped his forehead. "Political contributions and art! Why didn't I think of it? I saw a piece about it on the news last week."

George frowned. "You guys are losing me."

"If Ken and Connor are involved in the kind of

deal that was described in the news segment," Mick said, "they managed to make a political contribution to Watanabe by buying the van Gogh from him at a five-million-dollar mark-up. Watanabe bought the painting for ten million, and then got fifteen million for it from Ken and Connor—leaving him with a cool five million."

"That's got to be it!" Nancy said, grabbing his arm excitedly.

George shrugged. "I don't understand. Why bother with the van Gogh? Why not just give Watanabe the five million outright?"

"Because there's a limit on political contributions in Japan," Mick explained. "Carrying out the two van Gogh transactions through Nobu Auctioneers would have enabled Watanabe, Ken, and Connor to beat that limit."

"Wow," George said. "That's pretty clever."

"There's another benefit to a scheme like that," Mick continued. "It not only keeps the contribution secret from the authorities, but from the public, too. Politicians don't like the public knowing that any particular individual or corporation is giving them tons of money. It looks bad, makes people think that the politician might be giving special favors in exchange for the money."

"But what favors would Ken and Connor have gotten from Watanabe in exchange for this huge contribution?" Nancy asked.

Mick shrugged. "It might have been something

specific, like getting some law passed that would benefit Nakamura Incorporated. Or maybe they just wanted to have a very good friend in the government, for future use."

Nancy took another bite of her noodles. "I think we're on to something. This theory would explain a lot of things—the five-million-dollar difference in Watanabe's buying and selling price, why he unloaded the painting so fast, why his name was left off the Nobu bill of sale—"

"And why Nakamura Incorporated's identity as the buyer was confidential information," George added.

"It would also explain last Thursday evening," Nancy said, waving her chopsticks in the air. "Imagine this. For whatever reason, Connor happens to leave the wrapped van Gogh in the executive conference room for a moment. He comes back to get it, and sees Midori unwrapping it. He knows she's a big art buff, and he's afraid she might recognize the painting. He's also afraid she might just happen to know about Watanabe's purchase of the very same painting a couple of weeks earlier.

"So Connor's worried about Midori putting two and two together," she continued. "He goes running into Ken's office to tell him what happened. A few minutes later Midori goes to Ken's office, too, and overhears them discussing her."

Mick drummed his fingers on the table. "I bet that's exactly what happened. Midori was the big glitch in their scheme, and they were prepared to take care of her rather than face major jail time."

Nancy narrowed her eyes. "But what if there was another glitch—a glitch involving Connor?" she said. "Maybe something went wrong, and Ken ended up having to take care of him, too."

"I don't like the sound of that," George moaned. "If Ken was desperate enough to kill his partner, what's he capable of doing next?"

"Good point," Nancy said grimly. "I think we'd better wrap this case up before Ken gets a chance to hurt anyone else."

Out on the sidewalk, Mick bid Nancy and George goodbye. "I've got to get back to the office and finish up a few things," he said. "Can I meet you someplace in an hour or so?"

"George and I should head straight for Mad Dog's and warn him and Midori about Ken," Nancy said. "Why don't I call you later at home?"

Mick nodded. "Sounds good. Please be careful, okay?"

"You be careful, too," Nancy told him. "For all we know, Ken may be on to you, too."

After Mick left, George turned to Nancy. "Cab?"

Before she and George could get one, they ran into Mari.

Mari broke into a happy smile. "Nancy! George!

What a coincidence! What are you doing in Akasaka?"

"Meeting a friend," Nancy replied quickly. "What about you?"

"I was up at Nakamura Incorporated to see Ken," Mari explained. "My parents wanted me to give him some papers having to do with the canceled wedding." Then she blushed deeply and stared down at the ground. "Listen. I owe you an apology."

"What for, Mari?" George asked.

Mari looked up. "I broke my promise," she confessed. "You see, Ken and I were talking about Midori, and he seemed really upset about her still being missing. I felt so sorry for him that I ended up telling him where she was."

Chapter

Fifteen

YOU TOLD KEN where Midori was hiding?"
Nancy repeated, horrified.

"I know she didn't want anyone to find out,"
Mari said weakly. "But Ken seemed so depressed. And I thought the two of them might be
able to patch things up once they saw each other
again and had a long, heart-to-heart talk."

"Excuse us, Mari, we have to make a really
important call," Nancy broke in. "We'll explain
everything later." She grabbed George and
pulled her toward the phone booth, leaving a
puzzled-looking Mari standing on the sidewalk.

"Do you think we're too late, Nan?" George
said nervously as she closed the glass doors of the
booth behind them.

Nancy dialed Ken's number at Nakamura Incorporated. "I hope not," she replied.

There was no answer.

"Do you think Ken's on his way to Mad Dog's?" George asked anxiously.

"You can bet on it," Nancy murmured. She picked up the phone again and dialed Mad Dog's number.

"Busy signal," she grumbled, hanging up. "Listen, George—we can't waste any more time. I'm going over to Mad Dog's to warn them about Ken."

"I'm going with you," George insisted.

Nancy shook her head. "I want you to go to Nakamura Incorporated and get Mick. Or call him from here and wait for him. Then bring him to the studio with you as soon as you can."

"Are you sure you'll be okay by yourself?" George said doubtfully.

"I'll be fine," Nancy reassured her. "It's Midori we should be worried about."

As Nancy got out of the cab in front of the vacant lot with the sagging fence, she spotted an expensive-looking black sedan parked halfway down the street.

That must be Ken's, she thought anxiously.

Nancy sprinted across the lot toward Mad Dog's building. She reached the security door and was about to open it when she heard voices coming from the other side.

One of them belonged to Ken. "You know

what to do," he was saying gruffly in Japanese. "They're in the second-floor studio. They may be expecting trouble, so be very quiet on your way up."

"Right, boss." It sounded like the voice of a young guy. Nancy didn't recognize it.

Nancy heard someone step toward the door. The knob began to turn. Thinking fast, she raced around the corner of the building and crouched down low.

The door creaked open. Nancy edged her hands along the brick wall of the building and peeked out. Emerging from the doorway was the tall, slender, well-dressed figure of . . . Seiji Nakamura.

Nancy gasped. What was *he* doing there? She'd heard *Ken* speaking, not his uncle!

Then it dawned on her. Seiji and Ken had very similar deep, husky voices. She recalled noticing it at the Hamada Imperial Villa when she first met them.

As Nancy watched Seiji crossing the lot, something else dawned on her. Perhaps Midori had overheard *Seiji* scheming with Connor in Ken's office last Thursday. The office door had been closed, Midori had said.

Nancy shook her head in amazement. Was Seiji Connor's partner in crime—and killer? Had Ken been innocent all along? Where *was* Ken, anyway? And where on earth was Seiji going?

Then Nancy remembered the young guy who was on his way up to Mad Dog's studio.

"I've got to stop him," she said to herself, and crept around the corner of the building. Seiji had headed out to the street and had his back to her. She ran to the security door, opened it with her credit card, and dashed inside.

Once in the dimly lit concrete hallway, Nancy stood very still and listened. What was going on? she wondered. Was the guy already in Mad Dog's studio? But then she heard the faint sound of footsteps above her and to the left. He must have just reached the upstairs landing, Nancy guessed.

A plan began to form in her mind. It would be risky, she thought, but definitely worth a shot if she was going to save Mad Dog and Midori.

Nancy glanced around and found what she was looking for hanging next to the door—a fire extinguisher. Moving speedily, she opened the security door and let it fall shut with a bang, grabbed the fire extinguisher, and planted herself in a small, dark corner behind the foot of the stairs.

She closed her eyes briefly and tried to concentrate on what she would say next and how. She had to speak perfect Japanese, with no American accent whatsoever, and imitate Midori's nervous, high-pitched voice, to boot.

It was now or never. "Mad Dog!" she called out suddenly. "I think someone's upstairs. Let's get out of here."

Nancy opened her eyes. Her hands, which were gripping the fire extinguisher, felt sweaty.

Almost immediately, Nancy heard footsteps moving softly and swiftly down the stairs. She instinctively retreated farther into her shadowy hiding place. In another second the man was at the bottom of the stairs. He hesitated and looked around warily.

Now! Nancy told herself, and swung the fire extinguisher at the back of his head.

He let out a moan and crumpled to the floor. He was young, and he had a crew cut.

"You!" Nancy muttered out loud. It was the guy who'd thrown the deadly *shuriken* at her and pushed her into the bonfire at the Bon Matsuri festival! And he was most likely the one who'd delivered the poisonous fugu.

She realized that she would have to leave him there for the moment. She had to warn Midori and Mad Dog about Seiji.

Nancy set the fire extinguisher down and dashed up the stairs two at a time. When she got to Mad Dog's door, she stopped and listened. She could hear Midori and Mad Dog carrying on a conversation in hushed tones.

Nancy banged on the door. The conversation stopped abruptly.

"Midori! Mad Dog! It's me, Nancy. Please let me in!" she shouted.

The door opened. Mad Dog was standing there, his hair disheveled.

"You missed all the action," he told her drily. "Midori's fiancé dropped by just a few minutes ago."

Midori rushed up to Mad Dog's side. Her eyes were filled with tears, and her cheeks were flushed. "Everything's such a mess, Nancy," she murmured. "Ken managed to find us!"

"I know," Nancy replied, walking into the studio. "George and I tried to—"

"You knew about Ken?" Mad Dog cut in, his dark eyes flashing. "Why didn't you warn us? We were sitting ducks."

"We tried to call you as soon as we found out about Ken," Nancy said patiently. "But your line was busy, and Ken was on his way here. I jumped into a cab and got over here as soon as I could."

"He's in the bathroom," Midori said.

Nancy looked confused. "What?"

"I didn't even want to let him into the studio, but Mad Dog said he wanted to take care of him once and for all," Midori explained. "He opened the door and punched Ken in the jaw, just like that."

"He was out cold. We locked him in the bathroom," Mad Dog added. "We were just getting ready to call the cops when you showed up, Nancy."

"Oh, boy." Nancy took a deep breath. "Listen, I have some big news for you both. Midori, remember when you overheard Ken talking to Connor last Thursday?"

141

"How could I forget?" Midori said miserably.

"Well, that wasn't Ken you heard," Nancy said. "I know you thought it was, but it wasn't. I just figured it all out a few minutes ago—"

She stopped talking. She realized that Midori and Mad Dog were no longer listening to her and were staring over her shoulder at something.

Nancy turned around. Seiji was standing in the open doorway, a gun in his hand and a blood-chilling smile on his face.

Chapter

Sixteen

KEEPING THE GUN POINTED at Nancy and her friends, Seiji kicked the door closed behind him.

"I'm so glad to find you here, Ms. Drew," he said silkily. "It'll make what I have to do so much easier. What's that expression you Americans have? Killing two birds with one stone? Except that in this case, it'll be three birds, won't it?"

Midori was the first to speak. "But I don't understand," she said, her voice trembling. "What are you doing here, Mr. Nakamura?"

"I was just about to tell you," Nancy said slowly. "It was him, not Ken, you overheard talking to Connor last Thursday."

"What!" Midori gasped.

Seiji continued to smile his eerie smile. "Please go on," he said. "I would be most inter-

143

ested in learning the fruits of your detective work, Ms. Drew."

Nancy proceeded to explain to Mad Dog and Midori what she had discovered about Seiji, Connor, and the politician, Watanabe. "That's why Connor was so upset when he saw you unwrapping the van Gogh, Midori," she finished. "He was afraid their little scam would be revealed."

"Very good," Seiji said, giving Nancy a little bow. "You're really quite resourceful. You would have made a marvelous addition to Nakamura Incorporated—it's a shame I'll have to kill you."

Nancy felt goose bumps prickling her arms. Stay calm, she told herself. Buy yourself some time. George and Mick will be here soon.

She looked at Seiji levelly. "You're quite resourceful yourself. Coordinating the van Gogh transactions with Watanabe through Nobu Auctioneers must have been quite a challenge."

"It wasn't the first time," Seiji said, shrugging. "I've made many such transactions in the past year, with the help of Connor and my contacts at Nobu. Thanks to them, I have many good friends in the government. Friends who are willing to, shall we say, pull strings for me."

Midori shook her head and glanced toward the bathroom. "I can't believe I suspected Ken."

"I didn't know of your suspicions about my nephew," Seiji said to her. "Of course, I didn't know until now that you'd eavesdropped at his door at such a crucial moment and mistaken my voice for his."

"Where was Ken while that was going on?" Nancy asked curiously. "Why were you and Connor in his office, but not him?"

"Ken and I were having a meeting in his office," Seiji explained. "After Connor found Midori with the van Gogh, he came rushing in and asked to have a word with me in private. Ken offered to leave us alone for a few minutes—he said that he had to go see Gil Armstrong about something anyway."

While Seiji talked, Nancy began sneaking glances around Mad Dog's studio. She needed a backup plan in case Mick and George didn't make it in time.

"Your fiancé knew nothing of our activities, Midori," Seiji went on. "Otherwise, he wouldn't have told me where you were hiding."

"He told you?" Midori cried out.

"I ran into him just outside my office about an hour ago," Seiji said. "He looked very excited. When I pressed him for an explanation, he said that he was on his way to this address to try to win you back."

Midori turned pale. "Oh, no," she murmured. "My poor Ken—"

"I never dreamed of including my nephew in the scheme, Midori," Seiji said, sighing. "I always sensed that he disliked me. I knew I couldn't trust him."

"Speaking of trust, why did you kill Connor?" Nancy said suddenly, hoping to bait Seiji into a confession.

Midori and Mad Dog looked amazed, but Nancy just shook her head.

Seiji glared at her. "What makes you think I killed him?" he said coolly. "Well, never mind, you won't be around to cause me any trouble anyway. Yes, I killed him. Or rather, I had Shin do the job. You know Shin, Ms. Drew. He was supposed to come up here to scout things out while I went to the car to get my gun. But thanks to you, he's lying unconscious downstairs."

"Well, thanks to him, and you, I was nearly poisoned by a piece of fugu, and pushed into a roaring bonfire, and sliced up by a *shuriken*," Nancy snapped.

"You'd become most inconvenient," Seiji said simply. "You see, I wasn't terribly worried about Midori until she ran away from the wedding. Then I feared she suspected something about the van Gogh. But I thought she would stay in hiding. If she resurfaced, I planned to silence her with threats."

Midori shuddered. Mad Dog moved closer to her and put his hand on her shoulder.

"When I learned that you were searching for Midori, Ms. Drew, it was obvious to me that you had to be stopped at any cost," Seiji continued. "You're a detective. There was a chance you would get to the bottom of my little art transactions."

Nancy spotted an open bucket of paint on the floor, behind Seiji's feet.

Seiji glanced at her suspiciously. "Am I boring you, Ms. Drew?"

"I was just thinking," Nancy said quickly. "You must have really started getting nervous when Ken caught me at Connor's Rolodex."

"My nephew happened to tell Connor your ridiculous story about trying to find some woman's name in it," Seiji said. "We realized at that point that you were getting much too close to the truth. Then, early this afternoon, the accountant at Nobu called Connor and wanted to know if his lovely American secretary had gotten the van Gogh papers to him in order."

He paused, then added, "Courage was never Connor's strong suit. Right after that phone call, he marched into my office and told me that he wanted out before you had the authorities at our doorstep, Ms. Drew."

"So you punished Connor for his lack of courage by having him killed?" Mad Dog spat out.

"I also wanted to make sure he would never be able to testify against me, if it ever came to that," Seiji replied glibly.

His eyes glittered behind his rimless glasses as he raised his gun higher. "And now I will have to kill the three of you," he announced. "I plan to make it look like your handiwork, Mr. Hayashi. I can see the newspaper headlines now: 'Crazy Artist Shoots Friends, Then Turns Gun on Himself.'"

Midori covered her face with her hands. Nancy stared at Seiji—then happened to notice a figure behind him.

It was Ken. He had somehow managed to get out of the bathroom and was moving silently toward them.

"There's just one problem with your plan, Mr. Nakamura," Mad Dog burst out suddenly. "A big problem." Nancy realized that he had noticed Ken, too, and that he was trying to stall for time so Ken could get to his uncle.

Trying not to attract Seiji's attention, Nancy fixed her eyes on Ken's and cocked her head very slightly to make him notice the open bucket of paint behind Seiji's feet.

Ken saw it. As soon as he was close enough, he reached down quickly, picked up the bucket, and flung its contents over Seiji's head. Bright blue paint splattered everywhere.

Seiji cried out in surprise, and his gun went off. The bullet ricocheted off the ceiling. During that crucial split second, Nancy reached for the closest weapon she could find—a table lamp. She picked it up and brought it down as hard as she could on Seiji's gun hand. Seiji dropped the gun, and it skittered across the wood floor.

Seiji flung his paint-covered glasses off and dove for the gun, which had ended up near one of the vinyl lawn chairs. Ken went for it at exactly the same moment.

Seiji got his hand on the gun first. He rolled over to face Ken and raised it ever so slightly in the air, just inches from Ken's head.

"No!" Midori screamed.

In his frenzied attempt to retrieve the gun, Seiji hadn't noticed Nancy coming around behind him. Before he could pull the trigger, she leaped forward and ground her heel down on his gun hand. He yelled out in pain, and his fingers fluttered open, releasing the gun. Nancy bent down then and yanked Seiji's right arm back into an immobilizing half nelson.

"You're finished," Nancy told him breathlessly. "And you and your crooked friends are going to jail for a very long time."

Mad Dog picked up Seiji's gun and dropped it into what was left of the bucket of paint. Midori burst into tears and ran into Ken's arms.

He held her tightly. "It's okay," he whispered into her hair. "It's over."

Just then, George and Mick came racing through the door. They stopped and stared at the scene with their mouths hanging open.

Finally George said, "What did we miss, a finger-painting party?"

Nancy entered the enormous white tent on Mick's arm. George and Gil followed close behind, laughing loudly about something. Much to Nancy's surprise, her friend had taken a liking to the brainy Australian.

Inside, about a hundred people were milling around. Waiters in tuxedoes drifted by, balancing trays of hors d'oeuvres and champagne glasses high in the air.

"Leave it to Yoko Nakamura to throw a party together on four days' notice," Nancy remarked. "This is great."

"It's almost as great as the wedding ceremony was," George said. "I loved that poem Ken wrote for Midori—it was so romantic!"

"It was nice that they decided to hold the whole thing here, at the park where they had their first date, rather than at the Hamada Imperial Villa," Mick added. "That place would have reminded them too much of Seiji Nakamura."

Gil took a piece of shrimp sushi from a passing waiter and said, "So our once-esteemed boss has been incarcerated, eh, Mick?"

"Yup," Mick replied. "His sidekick, Shin, is in jail, too. And so are Watanabe and a bunch of Nobu employees."

"But Mrs. Nakamura managed to arrange to

keep the whole thing out of the papers until tomorrow," Nancy added. "As far as most of these wedding guests are concerned, Seiji Nakamura is on an overseas business trip." She paused and chuckled. "It's ironic that after everything Ken's mother ended up coming through for him and Midori. Finding out what they had suffered on her brother-in-law's account really turned her around."

"Ken and Midori definitely deserve a happy ending," George remarked.

Nancy sipped some sparkling cider and studied the crowd. She spotted Ken's mother, Mari, and Midori's parents. She also noticed Hana and the three teens from Café Vertigo, dressed from head to toe in black leather. Someone was missing. . . .

"Where's Mad Dog?" she said suddenly. "I didn't see him at the ceremony. Did any of you?"

George, Mick, and Gil looked at one another, then shook their heads.

"I can't believe he'd miss the wedding," George said, perplexed. "Where could he be?"

They heard the deafening roar of a motorcycle outside the tent. A few moments later Mad Dog came rushing in. He was wearing a black and pink polka-dot tie in addition to his torn jeans and leather vest.

He saw Nancy and her friends and came up to them. "My bike broke down in the middle of the highway," he said, panting. "I had to spend an hour fixing it. I hope Ken and Midori aren't furious at me for missing the ceremony."

"How could we be furious at you, Mad Dog?"

Nancy turned around. Midori was standing a few feet away. She looked radiant in her white silk kimono embroidered with gold cranes and flowers. Ken was at her side, his arm around her waist.

"I don't think I've thanked you yet for taking care of Midori," Ken said, extending his hand to Mad Dog. "I hope we can be friends."

Mad Dog grinned and clasped Ken's hand. "Absolutely."

Midori fixed her amber eyes on Nancy. "We owe our deepest debt of gratitude to you. If it hadn't been for you, this wedding would never have happened."

"Oh, I don't know about that," Nancy replied, blushing slightly. "When two people are meant to be together, they always seem to find their way back to each other."

"That goes for friends, too," Mick said, gazing meaningfully at Nancy. Then he raised his glass in the air. "I'd like to propose a toast to Midori and Ken. May they have a lifetime of love and wonderful adventures together."

Everyone clinked glasses. In the background the orchestra began to play a lively melody.

"I think that's our song," Ken said to Midori, and they sailed off to the dance floor.

"Nice toast," Nancy whispered to Mick.

He grinned. "To tell you the truth, I kind of meant it about us, too. Not the lifetime of love, but the part about wonderful adventures. What do you say we rendezvous every few years or so and tackle a case together?"

Nancy laughed and raised her glass. "You're on."

Nancy's next case:

The River Heights Falcons are vying for the Triple-A championship, and the team's hopes rest on the arm of Sean Reeves, recalled from the majors to pitch in the series. But from her front-row seat, Nancy can see that winning at baseball is the last thing on his mind. And she soon finds out why: He's fighting for his five-year-old daughter's life!

Sean has received a note that has left him no choice: "Lose the game or Caitlin dies." But Nancy uncovers a pattern of greed, deceit, and betrayal extending far beyond the baseball diamond. With time rapidly running out, Nancy knows that finding the true motive behind the crime is the only way to ensure that Caitlin, once again, will be safe at home . . . in *Squeeze Play,* Case #97 in The Nancy Drew Files™.